SILVER SEDUCER

Warriors of Valose Saga 2

IONA STROM
LS ANDERS

D1519293

❀ Created with Vellum

Also by Iona Strom

Nomadican Mates Series

Nomadican Mates Series Mega Box Set (books 1-7): Sci-Fi Alien Abduction Romance

Alien Intervention Romance

Zaku: Alien Intervention Romance book 1

Coming Soon!

Warriors of Valose Saga

Silver Savage: Warriors of Valose Saga 1

Silver Seducer: Warriors of Valose Saga 2

Silver Savior: Warriors of Valose Saga 3

Silver Solace: Warriors of Valose Saga 4

Silver Scout: Warriors of Valose Saga 5

Silver Silence: Warriors of Valose Saga 6

Silver Spice: Warriors of Valose Saga 7

Silver Storm: Warriors of Valose Saga 8

Silver Steel: Warriors of Valose Saga 9

Silver Stealth: Warrior of Valose Saga 10

More Warriors to Come!

Glossary of Valosian Terms

Special Note:

You'll find the following **Valosian** words throughout this text. They are not misspellings but alien terms. Also, they are no longer italicized since they seemed to have been a distraction for some readers.

This is an ever-growing list and may not have captured every single Valosian word. I'm currently working on it, so don't hate me for not being perfect.

Adrenalyne- A hormone secreted by the adrenal glands in males only, which increases strength, endurance, and stamina for the sole purpose of protecting their spirit mate. Also, this hormone promotes healing.

Chiksin- The Valosian equivalent of a chicken.

Crikts- Large insects that look like cave crickets.

Dearth- A herbivorous creature similar in size and look to a deer.

Electro-bars- Electrified bars of light.

Elksen- A herbivorous creature similar in size and look to an elk.

Fates- A Valosian measurement equivalent to a foot.

Fibrous tubing- Similar to fiberoptic cable.

Flites- Small flying insects that eat the dung of rexose.

Floratrap- Is a carnivorous plant similar to a Venus flytrap, only much larger.

Hipose- A herbivorous creature similar on size and look as a hippopotamus.

Hundredths- A measurement equivalent to a hundred.

Hurs- A Valosian equivalent to an hour.

Insectoids- Nuttaki species of insect-like mammals.

Kiltus- Similar in fashion to a Scottish kilt worn only by males.

Lood- Valosian equivalent to water.

Loodfall- The Valosian equivalent to a shower. This term can also mean a waterfall.

Luminetric barrier- Impenetrable transparent shielding.

Mims- The Valosian equivalent to a minute.

Milose- A Valosian measurement equivalent to a mile.

Mothis- A flying insect with fuzzy wings.

Munthis- A Valosian equivalent to a month.

Nula- Term of endearment like sweetheart.

Nutrillium- A mineral mined on Valose with the potential to release stored energy.

Nutrone- A rare mineral found only at the highest peak of the Jurigon Mountains.

Patooga- A large feline-like beast with enormous canine teeth.

Penitentrium- A building used to house prisoners.

Rovers- A mode of transportation similar looking to a jet ski, only they are used on land. They are equipped with gravity disruptors in order t hover above the ground and use thrusters to propel them forward.

Rynose- A herbivorous beasts similar to a rhinoceros.

Sanitate system- Is the Valosian equivalent of a toilet.

Sec- The Valosian equivalent to a second.

Skypod- A lightweight metal structure meant to float using a gravity disruptor.

Solaries- Rocks which absorb solar energy and emit light as from chemiluminescence of phosphorus.

Solitarium- Isolated prison cell.

Splinth- A clear shell used to set broken bones.

Spirits- Valosian Gods.

Squidlin- Massive carnivorous sea creatures with multiple tentacles.

Suns-fall- The time in the evening when the twin suns disappear and daylight fades.

Suns-rise- The time when the twin suns appear above the horizon as a result of the daily rotation of the planet, Valose.

Thrumming or thrum- Is a low continuous vibratory sound internally created by Valosian males to comfort or enhance pleasure.

Tondru- A massive wolf-like beast.

Tragore- A device used to detect power sources.

Turculine- Very close in hue to turquoise.

Yerons- A measurement of time approximately 365 days.

Acknowledgments

Proofreads and Edits by
Connie Lafortune
&
Owl Eyes Proofs & Edits

Cover Designed by Natasha Snow Designs
www.natashasnowdesigns.com

Map of Valose
RobDonovanauthor.com or
snikt5

Map of Valose

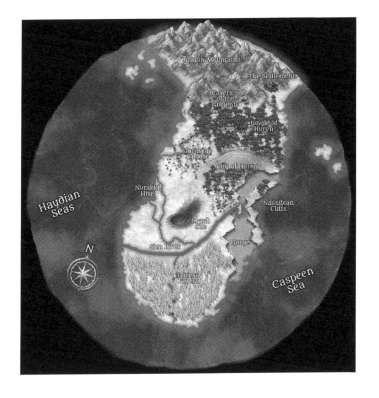

Chapter One

DRAGGAR

Sia Jakkar eyed me suspiciously as if he could hear the beat of my ancillary heart. It thrummed hard inside my ears; a rabid pulse needing to be answered.

The one that awakened me was out in the thick of the deadly jungle with my enemy. If the torn and bloody scrap of her dress fisted in my hand were any indication, she'd put up one serious fight. That was no surprise. My spirit mate was a warrior, like me.

My feet were planted firmly on the ground, but I was twitchy, waiting for Sia Jakkar's answer. My scales flashed blue and silver with my need to get out there and look for Marie as the last of the rynose pod was pushed out of the same hole in the settlement's wall they crashed.

"We can't leave the settlement open to the jungle, even though we are leaving it behind," Sia Jakkar stated.

"I want a repair crew on this wall now," Sia Jakkar's second in command, Nekko, barked out orders.

Males raced to do his bidding, not out of fear, but out of respect. We were preparing to evacuate. Now that the Gretolic had shown what they were capable of, the settlement was no longer safe. And safety was paramount now that we had females under our protection.

"You know I can't let you go alone, Draggar," Sia Jakkar stated flatly. "We need to call Aggar and Tekkon back from their current mission, now that we are relocating."

My eyes dropped to his shawra. I hoped to appeal to his recent awakening. The mark of his bonding still glowed softly from a recent joining of the spirits. His spirit mate, Lily, looked down on us, shifting nervously in the window high above in the safety of Sia Jakkar's skypod.

I prayed to the Spirits he would soften to my request to go after Marie and the other two females stolen from the settlement by Rayyar.

"You know in which direction they head, Sia," I implored. "Rayyar will use the females to gain entrance through the gates of Huren."

"Rayyar has a lead on you. You won't be able to catch him before he reaches the gates. Then how will you gain entrance? You're an exile, the same as me—the same as all of us." Sia Jakkar gestured to the males rushing around the settlement.

"Which means the longer I stand here, the more ground he puts between us." I placed my hand over the welt of my first bonding. "The recon mission has already been planned. Let me carry out that mission while I'm there."

None would have been more surprised than me when the sight of Marie had breathed new life into a heart that once beat for another. What I thought was dead was resurrected by the slight human female. She had proven to be as steadfast as any Valose warrior. I couldn't have asked for a better match.

We hadn't mated to initiate the bonding, so I lacked the echo of her spirit. I couldn't read her emotions. It terrified me not knowing if she was afraid or hurt.

My first spirit mate awaited me in the next realm, yet I

knew in my bones that Marie was mine. I'd never heard of a male having two spirit mates in a lifetime, yet the proof thudded behind my breastbone.

"I would prefer to ask for your permission rather than beg for your forgiveness." I squared my shoulders and straightened my spine. "I will go after her either way. And we need to know the status of Huren. Send me as recon, and I can place the scanner on the dome while I'm there."

"You are determined, aren't you."

Not a question. Sia Jakkar knew me all too well. "I have no choice but to act. She beats within me."

Sia Jakkar's eyes widened before he dropped his head with a curse. "Choose another to accompany you. Know that we are relocating to the Caverns of the Ancients. Take a rover. It will be impossible to catch up to Rayyar on foot."

"Thank you, Sia."

"I don't need to tell you to be careful." Sia Jakkar's gaze burned through me. "Valose cannot afford to lose you."

He didn't say the settlement or the human females we were protecting, but the *whole* of the planet. After recent events, didn't that just put things in perspective?

"I will see you at the caverns." To show respect, I presented my forearm for him to clasp. "I'll be taking Trisso as my second."

"Do not leave here without a comm."

"I won't." My words still hung in the air as my feet flew across the broken road to find our resident technology guru, Zikkar.

On the way, I found the companion I sought. Trisso, a craftsman who was also a budding warrior, I knew he would jump at the chance to exercise the fighting skills I taught him.

After a quick lesson from Zikkar on how to activate the scanner—armed with a comm and swords—Trisso and I rode together on our shared rover through the open gate as the rays of the twin suns rose higher above the horizon.

No longer our home, I didn't look back at the settlement. Everything had changed when the Gretolics showed their hand. We were gearing up for the battle of our lives, but first, I had to save Marie.

Chapter Two

MARIE

My head had never hurt this bad, not even when we crash-landed in the spaceship that had abducted us from Earth. I bounced on a wide shoulder, my body as limp as a wet noodle. Something dripped in my eyes—the tinny scent of my blood, the culprit.

I knew who was carrying me like a sack of potatoes. Rayyar. The enemy of the Valose males that rescued us from our abductors.

I fell into his clutches after Layla had grown some lady balls and slid down the rope of the skypod where we were all supposed to be sleeping.

She had snuck out, thinking we were all asleep. I'd kept quiet in the dark of Aggar's borrowed skypod, waiting until she made it to the ground and followed her.

Tiptoeing through the settlement in her Gucci shoes and matching handbag, the stupid bitch had freed Rayyar from his prison in exchange for an escort to the city of Huren. I had no idea what it was she hoped to accomplish by going there. Granted, it was beautiful—a gleaming city with tall buildings nestled under a shimmering dome.

If it was safety she was after, she was barking up the wrong tree. The Gretolics, those alien a-holes that abducted us to begin with, had taken over the city.

Maybe she was too good to stay inside the war-torn settlement. Or maybe, it was a combination of her blonde hair and the fact that we were all a little lightheaded from the oxygen-rich atmosphere that she'd pulled that dumbass move.

The fidiot was walking us right into the lion's den!

My stomach slammed down on solid muscle and bone as Rayyar leaped across something wide. Every particle of air left my lungs with the crunch. More blood dripped, and I swiped it away, managing to pry open my matted eyelids.

It was still dark out. The ground beneath me moved fast under Rayyar's booted feet. I glanced around to get a bead on where in the hell I was. I couldn't see much of anything from my upside-down predicament. I struggled to lift my body. That earned me a hard slap on the thigh.

Red hair flagged out beside me. I turned my head to find Amy in the same position on the opposite shoulder.

"Wake up, Amy!" I yelled and struggled against my captor.

"Stop moving, or I'll bash you in the head again," Rayyar cursed.

I understood every word he said, so my translator was still in place behind my ear.

Amy was Lily's fiery-headed bestie, the girl I befriended back on the spaceship. I envied Lily's resolve. She had been so courageous when I couldn't have been, venturing out on her own into God only knew what. She'd even chopped off some alien's hand that was, apparently, still alive.

Here, I found myself a captive once more. It was time to take a page from Lily's book and woman up.

I swatted at Amy's flailing arms with no response. She was either dead or out cold. I twisted my head around and caught a glimpse of the King Kong-sized wall around the settlement off in the distance.

This was good. I had a landmark.

Now to figure a way out of Rayyar's clutches. I wriggled more, craning my body up and around to get a better look at the jungle. There were tons of huge creatures with giant teeth that wanted to eat me living out here.

It was still dark, and in the short time I'd been on Valose, I learned most of the animals were nocturnal. I didn't see anything around except thick foliage.

Rayyar slapped me again. "Stop moving around, female, before I drop you."

A proverbial light bulb switched on over my head, a devious smile crept across my face, and a plan began to form. Rayyar had two girls slung over each shoulder. If I struggled hard enough, Rayyar would be knocked off balance. Once he lost his grip on me, I could take off into the jungle and run towards the settlement wall. I'd be instantly lost in the lush foliage.

This could work, or I could find freedom only to be swallowed whole by a giant jungle creature. Yet, if I did nothing, and Rayyar made it inside the dome covering the city of Huren, I'd be screwed, along with Amy.

Decision made; I forced my body to relax, giving the impression of compliance. I could use the element of surprise to free myself.

Like a ragdoll, I hung limply off his shoulder with my limbs flopping around. When I thought he was off his guard, I struggled in earnest.

Rayyar lurched to one side, stumbled, and dropped to one knee with a harsh curse. His grip on me loosened—only for a second—but enough for me to scramble free.

Rocks dug into my knees. I ignored the pain and crawled

away until I found my footing. My legs wobbled, and my head pounded as I sprinted headlong into the jungle.

Before the foliage swallowed me up, I chanced a glance back. Rayyar was rising from the ground, repositioning a limp Amy over his shoulder. Layla stood open-mouthed, glaring at me as I ran away.

Fuck Layla. She could get what she deserved, but Amy needed help, and the only way I could do that was to make it back to the settlement and round up some warriors.

An image of Draggar's scarred face popped into my mind as I fought through the thick vegetation.

I swiped away more blood trickling into my eyes as my legs pumped beneath me and looked back to make sure Rayyar wasn't following.

The pull Lily felt for Jakkar—the one she'd tried to explain to Amy—was real. I didn't completely understand it, but I felt it pulsating directly behind my breastbone.

It hadn't been for Aggar, though, who I was instantly attracted to, but for the most boorish, surly Valosian warrior on the planet.

Draggar.

Always a loner, I wasn't ready to admit that I needed him. As I battled through leaves as big as me and twisted tree branches acting as nets, I was not only fighting to get help for Amy but fighting to get back to Draggar. I didn't understand why I needed to see his face once more, but I did.

Suddenly, I broke through a small clearing. I stopped and took a step back into the edge of the jungle. I knew better than to expose myself to anything flying overhead.

Valose had winged monsters called wetlocks that looked like dragons. I'd seen one swoop down and pluck a thousand-pound rynose from the ground as if it weighed nothing. I wanted no part of that shit.

I stood quietly and listened intently to the sounds around me. Something big snorted off in the distance, probably a rynose. They were plant-eaters, but dangerous if provoked to stampede.

A roar belonging to the Valose version of a T-Rex, a rexose, was followed by a sharp screech from across the clearing. Something just became an early morning snack.

"Glad that wasn't me," I mumbled.

I looked up at the brightening sky. The twin suns were rising, and the jungle would soon sleep. A strong breeze pushed at the canopy, rustling leaves and parting branches. The settlement's wall revealed itself off in the distance. It was only a glimpse of the top edge, but it was enough to point me in the right direction.

With all the nocturnal creatures headed to bed, I had a better chance of reaching the settlement in one piece than I did under cover of darkness. If I ran my ass off and stopped for nothing, I could make it.

I flew across the clearing, my arms and legs churning out the distance. There was so much more than just my life riding on me reaching the settlement. It was Amy's, too.

Blood from my head wound dripped into my eyes. My lungs burned from the exertion. Having someone else counting on me gave me the courage to keep running. I'd never been responsible for anyone else before. I was determined to prove that I could be as brave and selfless as Lily.

The ground started to grow spongy, and the blue earth grabbed at my bare feet. My progress slowed. I trudged onward, having nearly reached the end of the clearing.

What was solid became hollow, and my legs punched through the ground until I was buried to my waist.

I clawed at the crumbling ground, yet the more I struggled, the faster I sank. My mouth and nose clogged with dirt as I fought for breath. Just as soon as I thought I was going to be buried alive, my flailing hands hit something hard, and I grabbed hold.

It felt like a root of some kind. I used every ounce of strength I could muster to pull myself out, but the thing was slick and studded with thorns. I kept sliding, my hands not finding purchase, despite the thorns biting into my palms.

I struggled for breath, sucking back small pockets of air as my face was, ultimately, covered by dirt. This was it. After everything I went through, I was going to die having been buried alive.

My legs kicked free. I scissored them back and forth in the open space. The ground covering me from the waist up began to loosen until it broke free, and I was in a freefall.

I landed hard on my back with a thud that robbed my lungs of air. I fought to suck back the musty air and stared up at the hole my body made in the ground above.

I'd fallen into a weird tunnel. The earth was dug out in a perfect tube. I recalled hearing the males talking about a mineral called nutrillium, a power source that had to be mined. It looked like I fell into one of the shafts.

I wondered, as my vision wavered and dimmed, if I'd ever see the scarred face of my warrior again.

Chapter Three

DRAGGAR

The jungle whipped past at a blinding speed. Trisso and I had spotted a path of broken branches and two sets of footprints leading away from the settlement and in the direction of Huren.

One set was large with the same sole pattern as every other Valose warriors' boots. The second had been small, dainty—a female's footsteps.

Three females were missing in all: Layla, Amy, and my Marie. I knew which female was doing the walking. Vallon saw Layla unlocking the door to Rayyar's prison and setting him free.

I recalled the many questions Layla asked about the dome and the city within as I escorted the females around the settlement. She hadn't been the least bit interested in the crumbling ruins we passed pockmarked from the last Nuttaki war. No. The glimmering city of Huren was all she wanted to know.

Marie had called her a sn-obb. I wasn't familiar with the word but guessed at the meaning after Marie prattled on about how some people didn't appreciate what they had because they lived a privileged life.

Marie had then squeezed my biceps and smiled up at me with heated eyes, and I instantly forgot all about Layla. Or, the whole damn planet, for that matter.

Given the evidence around the pod of rynose that rammed the wall, had Layla somehow known about the diversion? Had Rayyar contacted Sakkar with no one the wiser? My scales flashed with unease.

The dome was growing closer, but still no sign of Rayyar or the females. Fuck! Were we too late, and they'd already made it inside the city?

The rexose roar was the only precursor to the hipose carcass being flung through the air. Rexoses' liked to play with their food by tossing a fresh kill up in the air to catch it with its razor-sharp teeth.

Trisso took the brunt of the hit where he rode behind me on the rover. I banked a sharp turn to avoid the rexose crashing through the jungle after its kill.

My timing was a sec too late. Even though the rexose was as surprised to see us as we were him, there was no avoiding his snapping jaws.

And just like that, Trisso was gone.

The rover spun out of control, flipping through the air, end over end. I held on with a white-knuckled grip, finally coming to an abrupt halt against the giant trunk of a thriose tree.

I stayed where I landed. The wind knocked from me. Every bone in my body felt like it was broken. I watched in agonizing horror as the rexose crunched down on bone that didn't belong to the hipose before tossing back its giant head and swallowing.

The need for retaliation nearly blinded me with an urge to attack the rexose. I needed to save Marie, so I clung to my warrior training. It was certain death for a single warrior to attack a rexose. If I had the backing of five strong warriors, we could have stood a chance of bringing the beast down.

I was the only chance Marie, and the other females, had of being found. Sadly, I couldn't risk my own life to avenge Trisso.

A fat drop of the rexose's white blood ran a trail the size of a river down one flank. The glint of Trisso's sword flashed in the early suns-rise, having been buried to the hilt in the beast's tough hide.

The rexose collected its hipose and ambled off with a hard limp, leaving a trail of blood in its wake. I smiled wide and chuckled.

The rexose wouldn't last long with that grievous a wound. Trisso had avenged himself by taking out his killer. The young male had gone out a warrior, and I knew the Spirits would welcome him within their fold.

With the rexose gone, the jungle went still and quiet. I lay a moment listening to my raspy breaths before forcing myself to my feet. My muscles protested as I stretched out my bruised limbs.

I was lucky to have lived through the crash. Now that Marie had awakened me, my body was made more resilient and healed faster, thanks to the shot of adrenalyne being pumped throughout my body by my ancillary heart.

I took in the carnage that was the machine. The rover was—as Marie would have said—fucked. It lay in three separate pieces, which made me thank the Spirits that my body hadn't followed suit.

My sore bones cracked and popped as I dropped into a crouch, searching the broken off section of the rover for the medic pack Nullar tossed me as I was leaving. I flipped off the lid and looked over the contents—typical remedies and bandages for battleground injuries.

I was quick about using the suture disc on the worst of my open wounds, closing them up fast. The sweet scent of blood was not something you wanted on you in the thick of the jungle.

I skipped over the pain meds. My mind needed to remain sharp if I were to pick up on Rayyar's tracks again.

The rexose flung me way off course. The city's dome now lay off to the side of my current position. I'd have to cross the loamy field stretched ahead of me to get back to Rayyar's tracks.

It was a risk taking the shortcut. Wetlocks were well-known for swooping down and picking off prey in open fields.

My swords secure in the harness, crisscrossing my back, I strapped the medic pack to my thigh along with my loodskin and a sack of rations before checking the cloudless sky for any patrolling wetlocks. I saw none.

My newly awakened ancillary heart pumped out the extra boost of adrenalyne through my veins needed to sprint across the open field in secs.

Thanks to Marie, her spirit had breathed new life into a heart I thought long dead. With one eye ahead of me and one on the skies above me, I quickly cleared the field.

As I parted the jungle's heavy foliage, a shock of bright color against a blue leaf caught my attention. It was blood belonging to the humans.

I swiped my finger across the spot, smearing it. I sniffed and growled. It belonged to Marie. I would recognize her scent anywhere.

I quickly scanned my surroundings for any sight of her. I paused and listened hard; my ears perked and swiveled to catch even the tiniest of sounds.

Breath held, I waited. Listening.

The brush of a carnivorous plant rustled its leaf. A jungle beast snored softly in the distance. The sweep of a wetlock's wings stirred the air with a gentle swoosh somewhere far away.

Then I heard it. Just barely above a whisper, but it was there—a female's gentle sob. It sounded like it came from below my feet. I scanned the spongy terrain and, to my left, a patch of disturbed soil.

I rushed to the site, carefully navigating the hole. Dropping to my haunches, I peered into the darkness. In a single blink, my dark penetrating lenses allowed me to see the female below.

"Marie!" Thank the Spirits. I found my female.

Chapter Four

MARIE

I was hallucinating. That was why Draggar's voice calling my name sounded so real. It was total wishful thinking on my part that I fantasized him dropping through the hole to land next to me in a crouch.

I had completely lost my mind when I felt his tentative touch brush my hair off my face. That was when I started to sob in earnest. Besides my injuries, my bones ached to have Draggar with me.

"Don't cry, Marie, I found you." Draggar's voice taunted me. "I found you."

I cracked my eyes open to the vision of the male I wanted to see the most. He was there, kneeling by my side, looking as beaten as I felt. I closed my eyes against the tease of my crazed brain.

I turned my head to meet the soft sounds of shuffling. Then fingers smoothed over my head wound with a hiss of words. "Rayyar will suffer for this."

Next came a soothing warmth. My pain, gratefully, subsided. More of my injuries were treated in the same fashion until I almost felt myself again.

I was slowly dying. I had to be. My pain was leeching out as I would soon draw my last breath.

I didn't want to die in this hole. I didn't want to die at all, even after all I'd been through.

My life had never been an easy road, but I made peace with the trauma my father had inflicted on my young mind a long time ago. Although I remained guarded and distrustful of people as an adult, I still didn't want my life to end. There was still so much left I wanted to do.

"Open your eyes for me, nula."

I'd heard Jakkar address Lily with the term. Best I could figure, it was the Valose equivalent to sweetheart or honey. I wasn't exactly sure of the meaning, but it was definitely a term of endearment.

It was certain; I was hallucinating while in death's grip. Draggar would never sweet-talk me. He was bristly and surly, never sweet.

Sleep tugged at me. I resisted the urge to pry open my eyes. I wanted to remain in fantasyland where Draggar was caring for me and sweet-talking me like I was someone special.

Calloused hands cupped my face. I jerked from the sudden contact. Then a strange melody vibrated around me, soothing me on the inside.

I reluctantly opened my eyes... *He was there!* Draggar was leaning over me. His bright silver eyes stared down into mine with concern etched on his ruggedly handsome face. Tears sprang and rolled down my cheeks in vertical rivers.

"Are you in pain?" Draggar asked. "Nullar told me how to cut the pain med dose for one as small as you. Do you need it? What can I do to help you?"

"I could use a kiss." My voice came out as a gravely mess.

Draggar's heavy brow rose to his silvery-white hairline, and that vibrating cadence amplified. He leaned down, and only when the heat of his mouth, so soft and full, scorched mine did I know for sure he wasn't just a figment of my imagination.

I stopped breathing until his lips left mine. To be sure I wasn't crazy, my palm landed between the glowing patterns marking his pecs that reminded me of tribal tattoos. He was solid and warm and... *vibrating*? The melody that stirred my soul was coming from him.

"How are you doing that?" I flattened my hand more firmly to his chest. "How are you even here?"

"It's called thrumming. My spirit sings to yours." Draggar breathed and placed his hand over mine. "I came to save you and the others. I found you. I *found* you."

Did I dare entertain the tingles in my heart over his words? He seemed relieved to see me, yet he had also mentioned the others, not just me. Then again, his eyes were filled with such reverence it rocked me to the bone. What was with all the vibrating stuff?

Oh, who was I kidding? He was part of a search party out looking for the missing girls. I just happened to be the first one he found. Draggar didn't have feelings for me. He'd never even smiled at me, only stared in that intense way of his.

I mean, look at what happened when I allowed myself to be attracted to Aggar. He'd up and followed Rose around like a lost puppy.

Lily had tried to smooth that over, saying he thought of Rose like a sister. *Whatever.* I knew better. I'd never been any guy's first choice, and apparently, I wasn't going to be on this planet either.

I was an idiot to open myself for more heartache. Relationships always began the same way for me. Everything was great in the beginning, a true love story. Then I'd figure out in some brutal way that I was used, whether for sex or money, usually both. I'd be left with an empty wallet and an even more empty chest cavity.

"You found me." I smiled at him weakly. "Now we have to go after Amy. Where's the rest of the search party?"

Draggar paused in his stroking of my hand covering his sternum. I took that opportunity to slide my hand free. The slight softening of his features solidified into the Draggar I knew as he sat back on his haunches.

"Dead." Draggar's answer had come out of left field, shocking me. "Eaten by a rexose."

"Who... Who was it?" As if *Jurassic Park* had spilled over into *Lord of the Rings,* my mind had conjured Aggar's legs sticking out of the mouth of the giant beast.

"A male named, Trisso." Draggar diverted his eyes away but not before I saw a sheen of sorrow light them up. "A budding warrior that was lost too soon. He'd met his demise as a warrior and earned his place among the Spirits."

I'd never held much in the way of faith, but who in the hell was I to dispute his beliefs? Given my crappy life, maybe I needed to find some of my own.

An awkward silence settled between us, Draggar fiddling with the medic pack. This was Draggar in the raw, mourning the loss of a friend. From what I'd learned so far about the scarred warrior, he was like me and hid his emotions.

I could respect that.

Draggar unfolded a metallic sheet that reminded me of a giant piece of aluminum foil. He gathered me in his arms, brushed the dirt from my back, and spread the sheet out on the ground before laying me in the center. He folded over the ends, making me into a tinfoil burrito. I was instantly warm.

"You only mentioned Amy," Draggar said.

"Layla's a traitor," I spat. "When she thought we were all asleep, she left the skypod. I followed her and watched as she unlocked Rayyar's cell. That's when the rynose rammed the wall, and Amy came running out of the medic bay. She followed Layla, and then Rayyar came out of nowhere and snatched her up. That's when I got involved, but Rayyar hit me over the head."

Draggar's growl shook the tunnel walls.

"My sentiments exactly." I snuggled into my tinfoil blanket. "Rayyar needs his ass kicked."

"Oh, I will be doing more than kicking him in the ass," Draggar gritted out. "We must find Layla as well."

"What in the hell for? She's the reason Amy and I are in this mess."

"Sometimes, the ignorant need saving the most." Draggar's reasoning was sound, but ignorance wasn't an excuse for being a stuck-up bitch. "Layla would have been treated like royalty simply because she is female. However, now that the Gretolics control the crown, I don't think anything good awaits her inside the city."

"Layla is one of those rich bitches with a sense of entitlement larger than this planet." I went to cut my hand through the air, but my metallic burrito held my arms inside. "No way is she going to stay at the settlement after she locked eyes on that shimmering dome." I tried and failed to move my arms again. "Feeling a little trapped here, Draggar." I struggled against the metal sheet.

Draggar smirked down at me while loosening my trappings. "The swaddle was meant to comfort."

"Maybe if I was a baby," I freed my arms, "but as an adult, it feels restraining."

Draggar's face went dark. "Old habits," he grumbled and turned away.

"What? Wait..." I sat up and scooted around to face him. "What do you know about swaddling babies?"

The shifting blues and silvers of his scales gave away his

dark past. Maybe I shouldn't pry, but I couldn't resist picking at this fissure he was presenting.

For some bizarre reason, I really wanted to know the Draggar beneath the rugged exterior.

"I had a nurseling once. A female." Draggar's face softened. He focused on a spot behind me in a wistful stare. "The germ stole her away."

"How old was she?"

"Barely one yeron old."

"What of the mother?" I didn't understand the surge of jealousy that tackled me from out of nowhere.

"Killed by a floratrap." Draggar indicated the scattering of scars from his face to his thighs. "I earned these trying to save her. I managed to cut away the tentacles, but it was too late. By the time I reached the pod that devoured her, she was already dead. I tried to hold onto her spirit, but I was too late."

My mouth went dry. For the first time in forever, the hardened barricade around my heart cracked wide open. Empathy poured out in a flood, drowning out my cynical side. And those scars that gave Draggar his menacing air transformed into badges of courage.

"I'm so sorry." Before I could think better of it, I took his much larger hand in mine.

Draggar squeezed my fingers. Grief mixed with longing flowed from those soulful, silver eyes of his and pierced my heart, leaving me unprotected from his attentions.

As much as I wanted to keep my distance, Draggar was appealing to my sensitive side, leaving me raw and vulnerable. I wanted so badly to grab hold of the lifeline he dangled in front of my face. He represented safety, security, and shelter against the shitstorm of both our lives that we'd somehow survived.

I wanted to take it, to hold onto something solid and

finally feel grounded. And I wanted him to be the one to give it to me.

Yet, every damn time I put my trust in someone, I always came away with fresh scars. I bore wounds beyond my years. I was the product of my life's experiences. None of them good.

I was a total head case when it came to men. My relationships had always turned sour. What would make me think Draggar would be any different? Alien or not, he was still a male.

Chapter Five

DRAGGAR

Marie accepted a small dose of the pain meds. I waited until I knew she fell into a healing sleep before searching the mine shaft where she'd fallen.

When I first saw her face from above, I jumped into the deep hole without a second thought or a plan of how to get back out. I cursed my stupidity.

Marie needed to be returned to the settlement before I could go after Amy and Layla. Since Trisso had the comm and the scanner when he was plucked off the rover by the rexose, I couldn't ping Zikkar for help. The rover was done, so we'd have to walk out of here.

We couldn't be in a worse situation.

As she'd fallen into the dead-end of a mine shaft, there was only one direction I could search. I glanced back at Marie resting on the ground, cocooned in the metaloid sheet. I wished with all my spirit she'd invited me to join her. As soon as the distance between us began to close, she pulled away, slipping her tiny hand from mine.

The spark of interest had been there; I felt the attraction

of her spirit to mine. Reluctantly, I let her go with a firm plan in place to nurture the growing ember between us.

I continued down the long stretch of the mine shaft. Going by the new supports, it had been recently dug out. I would have never suspected how far the shafts reached in search of nutrillium.

No wonder Marie fell into it, dug out this close to the surface. Yet the shaft was barren. The glowing mineral used as our primary power source was hard to miss.

Given Huren's protective dome's ongoing fluctuations, Sia Jakkar's theory that the mines were running dry might be true.

My blue blood chilled in my veins. If the dome failed, it would be an open invitation for the Nuttaki to attack. Huren would be left defenseless. The Valose warriors that chose to remain with Sia Sakkar in Huren had grown soft after ceasing their training in favor of technology to keep them safe.

Now we faced a new threat—one from the stars—which we knew little about or how to fight.

The Nuttaki had forever been our enemy. We had battled with them for so long; we knew their weaknesses and how they fought. All except for the last war. The one that decimated the settlement.

The Nuttaki had surprised us with a new weapon from unknown origins powered by nutrone, a mineral found in only one place on Valose—on the highest peak of the Jurigon Mountain range where Clan Jurigon made their home.

We'd long blamed that clan for its collaboration with the Nuttaki because of past boundary disputes. We'd fortified the settlement's wooden wall and lived on in the few underground facilities until Hexxus, Zikkar's educator, had discovered a new usage for the depleted nutrone spears the Nuttaki left behind.

That was when the new city of Huren was built, and an impenetrable dome was created to protect it.

It had been assumed the nutrone spears and bombs were a design provided by the Jurigon clan because where else would a race of humanoid insects obtain such high-tech weaponry? Then again, how would an outmoded clan of cave dwellers create such a thing?

It was all a mystery, yet now that the Gretolics made themselves known, it was all too clear an alien presence was the culprit. How long had the Gretolics been on Valose?

I peered down the long expanse of the tunnel before me. Even with my nocturnal lenses in place, all I could see was a pit of darkness. My skin crawled, knowing the network of mine shafts were our only way out. I wasn't familiar with the mines. It was a real possibility we'd get lost.

I turned back when the mine shaft failed to present an exit. Marie hadn't so much as budged from where she lay snuggled in the metalloid sheet.

As I quietly sat down beside her, she turned toward me in sleep. Her slender arm snaking out to possessively rest on my thigh.

Marie was intentionally suppressing the call of her spirit. Mine wept to join hers, but a union could not be forced. The longer she denied the pull, the more I would yearn to make her mine.

Marie let out a small sigh and scooted closer. Her head now rested where her hand once laid. With gentle fingers, I smoothed the tendrils of her dark mane spread out over my kiltus. Her sweet scent an unbearable tease.

If only she'd allow me to bury my face in the hollow of her throat and get drunk on her scent. That was impossible. I'd lose control and have her beneath me before she had a chance to deny me.

I slumped back against the dirt wall, my fingers playing in

the silky threads of her mane. I never thought I would ever find another female that would stir my blood.

It'd been so long since I felt anything except the burden of loss and the anger of sorrow that the awakening of my spirit made me feel buoyant in my skin.

It hadn't been this way with my first spirit mate, Nakkia. She had answered the call of her spirit, and we mated to become one. But my Marie was not of Valose, and she knew nothing of our ways. I would have to be patient and wait for her. That didn't mean I wouldn't try and seduce her along the way.

The light hurs was the best time to travel, but Marie needed rest for her injuries to heal. I wasn't in any better shape. The rexose attack had depleted my adrenalyne. Now that my ancillary heart had calmed after finding her, my energy was consumed.

I allowed my eyes to close, keeping my auditory system highly vigilant. Not even the slightest of sounds would go unheard.

Chapter Six

MARIE

I snuggled into the warmth of solid muscle. A delicious musk cocooned me, and I knew without opening my eyes who the masculine scent belonged to.

Draggar.

The ruggedly, gorgeous alien elf with silvery-white hair softer than a bunny's tail and smooth scales that flashed with his turbulent moods.

Without a doubt, he was a dangerous warrior. I'd seen him in action wielding his swords against a huge, cat-like beast called a patooga that drooled a toxin capable of paralyzing its prey.

All of us girls agreed it was Valose's version of a saber-toothed tiger—on *crack*.

Not even paralysis of his right arm had stopped Draggar from fighting the beast. Right after, he went out hunting alone only to come hauling ass back to the cave, where we made camp, with a dead animal in one hand and a giant wolf snapping at his heels.

There was a fine line between bravery and stupidity, and I still hadn't decided which side of the line Draggar fell. But the guy was a total barbarian. Which shouldn't turn me on so much, but it did.

I felt completely safe with him. *Almost.*

"Ohmygod, my heart..." I sighed as a sound asleep Draggar gathered me close, nuzzling the top of my head as if I were a prized treasure.

That traitorous organ pulsing my rapidly heating blood through my veins melted with his heavy sigh. How would I ever survive this?

I relished the feel of his heavily muscled arms around me —my body drinking in his incredible warmth. The weird metal sheet he burrito'd me in had loosened, so the top half of my body was pressed skin-to-scales against him.

One large hand skimmed down to the small of my back and farther to cup my ass, pressing my belly against the steel rod of his massive erection.

I ever so slowly moved my hand, pushing aside the metal sheet bunched around my waist so as not to wake him. It'd been a while since I had some cock action, and something about this alien jungle was making me horny as fuck.

Or it could just be the company I kept.

I'd first been attracted to Aggar, which pissed me the fuck off. Lust had always steered me in the wrong direction. But what I felt for Aggar was more like hero worship, since he was the one that ultimately freed all of us girls from our metal cages.

Draggar, on the other hand—I stifled a moan at the slow grind of his hips—Draggar had grown on me during our trek from the crashed spacecraft through the perilous jungle to the settlement.

His gruff exterior was nothing but surly, yet he was respectful and conscientious toward all the girls. He made sure everyone had food and water. We'd been packed like sardines in the bed of the hauler he was driving, and never once did he complain about stopping for pee breaks.

The scarred warrior we all feared the most had turned out to be a big ole grizzly bear with a marshmallow center. I suspected all the girls were a little sweet on him by the time our journey was over.

Right now, I craved what he was grinding in the apex of my thighs. My skin was tight, and my pussy was swollen. I needed a release from the constant state of low-level arousal I felt whenever I was in Draggar's presence.

Penial penetration was out of the question. Lily had already shown us the result of that in the form of a shawra— the swirling design scored into her flesh—that there were no one-night stands on Valose.

Sex with one of these big, silver guys were for keepsies. And I wasn't interested in anything permanent.

Draggar startled awake when I squeezed his firm ass. His pelvis continued to grind while his expression was one of confusion then surprise.

"Just touching." My voice shook with pent-up sexual frustration. "Only touching." I urged his pelvis to rub his delectable cock in just the right place.

I was so close. *Sooo* close.

I damned near panicked when Draggar pulled away to surge down my body, spreading my thighs wide. I was naked beneath my shapeless alien dress. I nearly came from the anticipation of his intense perusal of my glistening sex.

I trembled in fear. I wasn't sure what scared me the most —what he planned to do to me or to be capable of telling him no if he wanted to fuck.

I'd heard the guttural moans echoing off the rocks when Jakkar and Lily did the nasty at the pool where we made camp. I laid awake all-night fantasizing about what sex with

Draggar would be like. It frightened me how much I wanted to find out.

"So beautiful," he grumbled, then dove in and devoured me.

Devoured me!

His tongue drove to the center of my being. I was stuffed full of his undulating heat, leaving no part of me untouched. His lips sucked and pulled at my clit, stimulating every part of my pussy at once.

It was impossible to catch my breath through the sensory overload; I was panting so hard and fast.

What sent me over the edge was the sharp points of his fangs grazing across my labia. He could tear me apart with his vampire teeth alone. He was erotically dangerous, and what he was doing sent jolts of lightning through my veins.

The guy was a walking, talking sex toy with a mouth made for pleasure and a body made for sin.

Every muscle stiffened at once, and I contorted into an arched bliss. My screams echoed throughout the tunnel. Even after I relaxed, Draggar kept at me, licking and sucking my over-sensitized flesh until I was a puddle of quivering mess beneath him.

"You know," I panted, "I was never much for oral," I swallowed, trying to catch my breath, "but you've changed my mind."

The big silver bastard had the nerve to grin at me while licking my juices off his chin. "Showing off your amazing tongue? I think, yes. Now I know what I'll be missing when I find a way off this death planet."

Draggar's eyes narrowed, and he growled back an answer like the beast he was. My beast looked to be ravenous.

"Time to return the favor," I smirked.

Two could play at this game. Even though oral sex had never been my fave thing, I could suck a mean cock. I pushed at one beefy shoulder, and he flopped over onto his back without question.

I crawled up his body, his hands settled on my hips and squeezed the fleshiest part of me. Insecure with my figure, I'd always been a bottom-heavy hourglass, carrying a little too much weight on my hips and thighs.

My breasts were slightly more than a handful, but my waist was small. But when Draggar looked at me, I was stripped of my insecurities and transformed into something to be worshipped.

I reached for the hem of his kilt, pushing it up his thighs. His breath caught, but he didn't stop me. I swallowed hard with every inch of his skin I revealed.

His thighs were the size of my torso, heavily muscled and tight. At nearly seven feet tall, Draggar was a magnificent specimen of male.

It didn't matter that his skin was reminiscent of snakeskin or that it could camouflage—or even that he was mostly silver. All I knew was he turned me on like no other.

I pushed the fabric higher to mid-thigh. Just a little farther, and I would see his cock for the first time. I paused a beat before exposing him to the waist—then gawked at what I saw.

"Magnificent." I practically drooled over his alien anatomy.

His cock reminded me of one of those naughty dragon dildos I was never brave enough to order. It was layered with slabs of ridges and had a row of knots lined up along the top like a spine. I moaned, imaging those bumping against my clit while he fucked me.

I licked around the mushroomed tip. Fleshy and bulbous, my pussy clenched, imaging the feel of it parting me—pushing into me. Draggar swiveled his hips and clawed his hands into the blue dirt beneath him. His heavy sack drew up tight to his body.

Settled between his tremendous thighs, I looked up his body to find him watching me with a hooded gaze and a sexy sneer displaying his massive fangs. I sneered back, knowing this dangerous barbarian was completely at my mercy.

"Who's the seducer now?" I quipped.

Without warning, I engulfed the head of him between my stretched lips. Draggar jerked on a gasp, and I wrapped one hand around the base of his girth. With the other, I began a steady pump with a little twist at the base. I took as much of it into my mouth as I could, swirling my tongue around the tip on my upward stroke.

Draggar's big body stiffened and twitched beneath me as if he were holding himself in check. The grinding of his teeth ricocheted around the tunnel in a grating echo.

I glanced up at his face. His head was thrown back; his lips parted in the throes of passion. I was the one making him feel this good. Didn't that make a girl's head all light and giddy.

At first, I thought I imagined movement beneath my palm. When I lifted my hand from around the base of his cock, triangular-shaped flaps erected in ascending heights. I nearly choked on the effects that would have on my clit. No wonder Lily had been moaning like a whore in heat.

A fresh rush of wetness coated my thighs. I humped at the air while I worshipped his cock. It was so tempting to say *fuck it* and put his monstrous equipment to good use. The tip popped out of my mouth, and I whipped my dress off over my head, carelessly tossing it to the ground.

My mind flashed an image of Lily's shawra, which guided me to straddle one of his thighs. I needed something solid between my legs, and the exotic features of his alien erection were—for real—driving me wild.

I felt so dirty fondling my breasts while dragging my pussy up and down his muscled thigh. What happened on Valose stayed on Valose, and if I wanted to be a dirty girl, then I was gonna be one with Draggar.

Before I knew it, I was plucked from Draggar's thigh and pulled up against his solid chest. "Maybe not this suns-rise or even the next, but your sweet cunt will sheath my cock before this is over." He snapped his fangs at my throat, flipped me over and around, so my ass was in his face and his giant cock was in mine.

I wrapped my hands around his erection as he speared me with his tongue. I squeaked around his cock when he spread my cheeks to bury his face between my thighs. He ate at me, and I swallowed him—both of us giving as good as we got.

This was my first time in the notorious 69 position. I had to say; I liked it. I really really liked it.

It wasn't long before Draggar's balls tightened, and my pussy clenched around his probing tongue. His cock seemed to swell in my mouth as my core melted in a surging gush. Stars exploded behind my tightly closed eyelids. Draggar tensed, ready to pop.

Hot liquid shot down my throat. It was surprisingly sweet. I swallowed and lapped at his juices while frantically rolling my hips, chasing down another orgasm.

It was greedy of me to ride his face like a crazed slut, but he didn't seem to mind. He had a firm grip on my hips, with his face planted firmly into my soaked flesh.

I came on a muffled moan around the head of his cock. I had a death grip on his sex, which seemed to turn him on given his final spurt's grand finale.

My body went as limp as a ragdoll, and I collapsed on top of him. Draggar lifted me as if I weighed nothing, flipping me around to sprawl across his chest.

The lower half of his face glistened from my sex. He

didn't bother wiping me off him. It was like he relished having juices on his face.

The entire tunnel reeked of sex. I heaved a heavy sigh and snuggled into his big body. I could stay like this forever, feeling him breathing and listening to his hearts beat in tandem.

Hearts! As in two?

I raised my head and laid my palm over his sternum. "You have two heartbeats."

Draggar laid his palm over mine, scooting it to the left. "This heart pumps blood through my veins." He scooted my palm between the deep valley of his pectorals. He hesitated, locking his eyes with mine. "This heart pumps adrenalyne through my body, making me stronger, more resilient to injuries, and healing me faster. This heart beats only for you."

"Me?" I recoiled in shock over his explanation.

"From the first sec I laid eyes on you and caught your scent on the breeze, I knew you were *mine*." Draggar rolled me to my back. I ceased breathing when his big body nestled between my spread thighs. His pelvis stirred, rubbing his hardening cock against my slick center. "Your spirit stirred mine back to life. You awakened me."

I wanted to groan and cheer at the same time. *Me!* Marie Rollins breathed life into another's heart. Shit like this didn't happen to me.

I felt that same stirring in my soul. A swirling of something warm behind my sternum whenever Draggar was near and a yearning vortex of emptiness when he wasn't. This soulmate thing Lily swore was real, really was, and I could totally understand why she didn't want to leave.

I didn't have the fortitude to live on this planet. Behind every prehistoric jungle leaf, around every giant boulder, was something with razor-sharp teeth wanting to eat me. I couldn't handle being at the bottom of the food chain.

I knew it, with every fiber of my being—if he claimed me with that monstrous cock of his—I would never be able to leave this planet. Here I was laid open for the taking, his bulbous tip slipping and sliding between my labia, teasing my clit.

God help me; I wanted to ride that huge alien cock of his. I wanted to experience all his extra amenities.

I was spent just a second ago, but with every delicious drag across my sensitive flesh, Draggar was recharging my libido. All it would take would be a yes from me, and he wouldn't hesitate to give me a fucking I would never forget.

"I can see the fear in your eyes. Feel it in the center of my being," Draggar groaned, churning his hips in time with mine. "I won't mate you until you're ready. When I do... When I enter you nice and slow and thrust into you nice and deep—over and over again—you'll scream my name and beg me never to stop."

I came on a shudder. The friction from the deep ridges of his cock shot electric zings through my clit. His dirty words only added to my pleasure. Draggar would have no problem stuffing that huge cock inside me; I was that wet.

"So sweet," Draggar buried his face in the hollow of my throat and breathed deep, "and so responsive is my tiny warrior with the tight sheath."

Draggar pulled away suddenly and scooped my hips up from the ground to meet his mouth. In a long swipe, he licked me from stem to stern, delving his tongue in my pussy to suck at my juices.

I screamed from the invasion. It was a wonder, with all the noise we made, every animal in the jungle hadn't heard us.

"This is my cunt." Draggar cleaned off his lips with his tongue. "You are destined to be mine."

I cocked my head at him. "Have you ever considered relocating to Earth?"

Chapter Seven

DRAGGAR

I gave Marie my pouch of rations. She handed it back and settled in beside me, nibbling on a dried chiksin strip.

"What about you?" Marie peered up at me through a thicket of dark lashes. "You have to eat something, Draggar."

"I can go longer than you without sustenance," I declared. "My body is more resilient than yours."

"Are you calling me weak?"

The sparkle in her dark eyes told me she was attempting to provoke me. When we first met, I discovered she liked to tease, to get a rise out of me.

My spirit mate was a feisty little morsel, and I was sorely tempted to kiss the smirk right off her face.

"Your species is simply not as robust as us Valosians." I paused in my packing of what few items we would be carrying with us. "It was not meant as an insult but a fact of biology."

It was a shame I didn't have time to banter with her. She could wield that sharp tongue of hers as well as any Valose warrior could a sharp blade.

"We need to get moving," I said. "The mine shafts are the only way out, and I'm not familiar with the tunnels."

"Shouldn't we wait until sunrise? When it's light out, and all the scary as fuck animals are asleep?" She stood, straightening her crumpled dress.

"It doesn't matter. We're underground. The only way inside the nutrillium mines is through a single entrance located inside Huren's dome," I explained. "Sia Sakkar closed off all the other entrances to keep out pillagers and exiles."

Marie pointed up to the hole she fell through with a smug raise of her eyebrow. "And that?"

I huffed out a breath and wagged a finger at her. "You're too impish for your own good, tiny warrior."

"Would you have me any other way?"

"I would have you all kinds of ways if you'd let me."

Marie's cheeks darkened from their usual pale hue. "Well, there's no wham-bam-thank-you-ma'ams on this planet. As much as I hate to admit that I like you, I'm not ready to get hitched."

I blinked at the flurry of words I didn't understand, waiting for the translator behind my ear to provide the meanings. The language barrier wasn't the most difficult thing to comprehend; it was the verbal contradictions. She liked me but hated to admit it? What did that even mean?

"Never mind." Marie cut her hand through the air and tucked the medic bag under her arm. "Let's get going before something with gigantic teeth decides to drop through that hole and eat us for dinner."

We followed the tunnel I'd partially checked. The farther we walked, the more my belly filled with trepidation.

The shaft was barren. There were no residual traces of the white phosphorescent glow left behind of a successfully mined mineral. There was nothing but dark blue earth.

"Sia Jakkar was right," I mumbled, running my hand along the dirt wall as we traveled.

"Right about what?"

"The nutrillium on this planet has dwindled. If judging by this shaft, it very well could be depleted—"

The blood in my veins curdled at Marie's shriek. My swords rang out a metallic song as I pulled them from the holsters. I whirled in all directions, searching for the enemy that caused my spirit mate such alarm.

She tried to scale the wall, digging her little nails into the crumbling dirt. Her eyes bulging from their sockets as a nest of newly hatched crikts scurried past on spindly legs.

"I hate spiders!"

Marie's voice echoed through the tunnel just before she launched herself at me. With my swords still up and at the ready, she caught me around the neck and wrapped her legs tightly around my waist.

I didn't know what a sp-eye-dore was, but it must be something terrifying on her world. If her reaction to the infant ones was this severe, I could only imagine what it would be to one of the full-grown adults.

"Nula," I sheathed my swords and wrapped my arms around her frantic form, "the crikts are more afraid of you than you are of them."

"Oh, I seriously doubt that." Marie turned her head this way and that, searching the ground for more crikts.

"They won't harm you. They're simply looking for a way out—*Fucking* Helios!" I swore to the Realm of the Wicked. "That's it. That's how we'll find our way out of this maze."

"How's that?"

"We follow the crikts!" I took off running after the scurrying insects. "As soon as they hatch out of the dirt, they look for a way above ground then for a lood source."

"Do you mind if I hang up here?" Marie tightened her hold on me as I sprinted.

"Not at all. I'm enjoying the heat of your cunt rubbing against my scales."

I didn't stop my hands from reaching down to squeeze the rounded globes of her ass. My spirit mate had some meat on her bones, and I liked the extra cushion.

Marie instinctively rolled her hips, and I knew she would soon grant me entrance into her fiery sheath. I just had to be patient and keep at her.

"Are you deliberately trying to seduce me with your dirty talk?"

"Is it working?"

"No."

"Liar," I grumbled out a laugh. "I can feel the wetness of your response. Just say the word, and I'll drop my kiltus right here and mate you standing up."

"Is it only about your cock when it comes to me, or is there something more?"

I stumbled over my own feet. "Can you not feel it? The call of my spirit to yours?" I thrummed out the evidence.

"You did this before. This vibrating. When you first found me." Marie placed her palm to my chest. "What does it mean?"

"Thrumming," I said, speeding up to not lose sight of the crikts as the tunnel veered off to the left. "It's the song of my spirit to yours."

"So, you're telling me you're serenading my soul?" She sucked in a sharp breath. "Is that why I feel the swirling tug behind my sternum?"

It thrilled me that her spirit answered my call.

"If I'm going to get us out of here safely, I need to focus." I swatted her backside and forced my attention on the dark abyss of the tunnel ahead.

I strained to hear every sound. My ears perked and swiveled, fine-tuning my auditory system until I could hear even the taps of the crikts thin legs hitting the ground as they scampered ahead of us.

Marie giggled and traced her finger along the point of my ear. "How do you move your elf ears around like that?"

I shook off her hand. "I don't know what an ell-f is. Now stay still so I can focus, female."

"Female?" she recoiled with a sneer. "That almost sounded like a curse."

"I'm just trying to concentrate on the path ahead," I scolded. "You're distracting me, and now is not the time for play."

"How dangerous can an abandoned mine shaft be?" Marie scoffed, tickling the shell of my ear, making it twitch. "There's nothing else down here but us and those creepy spider things—"

My ears flattened against my head from Marie's shriek. The crikts scurried across my booted feet. Some even climbed my legs as they suddenly turned and rushed back in the opposite direction. What were they running away from?

A strange whisper from up ahead prickled across my scales—I stopped and whirled around—or was it coming from behind? Marie went stone still, clinging tightly to me. Even without her distraction, I couldn't tell where the sound was coming from. It seemed to be coming from all around us.

We couldn't go back. There was nothing there except the hole Marie had fallen through that was too high above our heads to reach, so I forged ahead. The whisper amplified to a dull roar; the ground tremored beneath my boots.

It had to be a mining team digging new tunnels in search of nutrillium, though it didn't sound like any excavator I'd ever heard. I moved cautiously ahead, not understanding why I hadn't heard the machine running long before now.

Illuminated rods ran along the walls of the shaft. I paused and touched the wavy bands of light bouncing between the two. My hand easily passed through.

I took one step and then another until we were through

the lights. The excavator's noise was bruising on this side—the light acting as some sort of dampener.

We reached a point where the tunnel split off into two. One was filled with the racket of the excavator, while the other appeared empty.

I took the empty route, running headlong into the darkness and right into a group of Gretolics. I skidded to a halt, my boots kicking up a cloud of dust. I pried Marie off me and shoved her at my back. With my swords unsheathed, I was ready to cut down the alien enemy before me.

"Drop the weapons, Valosian," one of the Gretolics demanded.

My arms began to drop of their own volition.

"No, Draggar!" Marie shouted from behind me. "Don't listen to them. Block it out! It's a trick. They're controlling your mind."

I shook off the will of the gray freak and took a step forward, ready to swing my razor-sharp blades in a wide arc.

"Drop the weapons," two Gretolics spoke at once.

A conflict raged within me. My mind told me to do one thing, but my warrior instincts told me to do another. I tightened my grip on the hilts even as the tips of my swords drooped toward the floor. The only thing keeping me from ultimately succumbing to their words was the screaming of my spirit to protect my mate.

"Drop the weapons and get on your knees." Another Gretolic joined the ranks to complete a trio.

My head pounded from the pressure to do as I was told. Energy leached from my muscles with every word they spoke. I dropped to one knee, my swords falling to my sides.

Marie's shouts might as well had been miloses away. When the three began to chant, both swords clattered to the ground, and my knees hit the dirt with a dull thud.

"No!" Marie shouted again.

Pride swelled within me for my spirit mate as my mind went blank.

Chapter Eight

I would have never thought I had it in me, but the need to protect Draggar was undeniable. With one of Draggar's heavy swords clutched in both my hands, I swung and connected with the Gretolic closest to me with a sickening *thunch* of bone and flesh.

The blade cut that gray bastard in half like a hot knife through butter. I gagged at the orange splash of guts and blood, then swung again at the next Gretolic that stepped too close. He also dropped like a popped water balloon in a gruesome puddle.

The third Gretolic moved in to intercept me. I swung, just barely missing his bulbous head. He got smart and stepped back before I could cut him down.

"Put down the weapon, female," the Gretolic hissed.

"Fuck off, freak! That mind control shit doesn't work on me." I rushed him as he scampered away. "Where you goin'? Get your ass back here and have some of this Valosian steel!"

I might have only been five foot two, but inside I was as tall as Draggar. I felt like a total badass with my borrowed sword dripping with orange goo as the gray alien turned tail and ran away like a little bitch. I also wasn't cocky enough to think that he wouldn't be back with reinforcements, and then we'd be fucked.

I turned my attention to Draggar, who was shaking his head as if to clear it. Guilt weighed heavily on me. This was all my fault. I'd been playing around, distracting him instead of taking our situation seriously. We wouldn't be in this mess if it weren't for me.

"Draggar." I crouched before him, so our eyes met. "We have to go now. Can you hear me?"

He nodded sluggishly.

"Come on, big guy." I tucked myself under one of his massive arms and did what I could to help him stand. "We have to get out of here before they come back with more."

I managed to replace one of his swords in the holster across his back and kept one in my hand in case I needed it again. It weighed a ton and impossible for me to lift one-handed, so the tip dragged across the ground as I turned us around in the opposite direction.

Going forward was no longer an option. We'd just have to figure out a way to scale the dirt wall and go back out the hole I'd fallen through.

"So proud of you." Draggar's robust voice had turned weary. "You swung my sword like a true warrior of Valose."

"Aw shucks," I snorted. "Just doing what I could to protect my man. Anyway, this was all my fault. I'm so sorry for putting you in jeopardy."

"The fault lies with me," Draggar scoffed. "I failed you. I should have fought harder against the Gretolic's mind control."

"Don't you dare take the blame for this. And you didn't fail me, so stop it with that shit."

Draggar was an enormous male who fought like a berserker. In my eyes, he was indestructible. As he stumbled before resuming his footing, I was apprehensive about our situation for the first time since he found me.

I had no doubts Draggar would have gotten us out of this. Had it not been for me fucking around, I know he would have.

We hadn't gone more than a few feet before five Valosian males confronted us. They weren't warrior-sized like Draggar, but they were giants compared to the human men I was used to.

I scanned the grim faces and was met with a dull gleam instead of the lively swirl of silver eyes. They reminded me of hypnotized people with no self-awareness. Their bodies and kilts were dirty, as if they'd been working the earth. I noticed, absently, that the roar of machinery had stopped.

As two Gretolics shuffled around behind the males, I knew they weren't here to lend us a hand. The Gretolics wore some kind of device on their whip-thin wrists. The words they spoke into it propelled the males forward.

Draggar tried to push me behind him. I was having none of that and sidestepped his arm. Not fully recovered, he swayed on his feet as he pulled the sword I holstered on his back free.

Both of us stood ready for battle. My sword was not held as high as Draggar's, but I was prepared to swing if I had to.

"May you find your place among the Spirits," Draggar muttered before he roared and swung his sword in a wide arc cutting through the first male to lunge at us. Blood hit the dirt walls in a grotesque splash. The male's body crumpled at Draggar's feet like a broken doll.

The Gretolics raised those bracelets to their thin lips and spoke again. The back of my neck prickled with awareness. I whirled around to meet a wall of Valosian males.

My sword was raised, two-handed, and over my shoulder like a baseball bat. I unleashed my inner cray-cray and started slashing and slicing at the air. "I got your six, baby!" I hollered to Draggar, holding back the new arrivals.

I must have looked like a little kid with my dad's sword, but I swung at the males, knocking them off their game with my wildness. Draggar grunted behind me. Blood splattered the back of my head as I took on the males dodging and weaving my sword.

A hand grabbed my wrist and freed my grip. My opposite wrist went limp, the point of the sword dropping to the ground. My arms were like noodles from welding the heavy weight.

Blue blood trickled from the wounds of the attacking males as I'd gotten in a few good slices, but my advantage was lost as many hands swarmed my body. I fought and kicked, not ready to give up.

"Draggar!" I screamed and wrestled as I was tackled to the ground.

My wrists and ankles were bound with wide silver bands. Then I was hefted up and slung over a shoulder. The males turned, and I screamed, wriggling my entire body. I didn't want to be separated from Draggar.

His silver head whipped around to meet my eyes for a brief second before he went back to fighting. Only this time, his controlled swings had turned frantic. He was always chanting to the Spirits before his blade found its mark. He cut his way through the males determined to take him down.

As the last male fell to Draggar's feet, he whirled around to run after me. I reached out my bound hands, tears streaking my face.

The Gretolics had doubled in number and were bearing down on him. Their shark-toothed-filled mouths chanting in unison for him to stop, yet it was the males holding me who came to an abrupt halt.

"Not you, idiots!" a Gretolic snapped. "Weak-minded fools."

I wrenched my body free and collapsed to the ground with a hard *thud*. The male who had been carrying me like a sack of flour didn't so much as look down. He was so focused on the Gretolics barking out commands that Draggar continued to fight against.

My warrior had stopped moving, vigorously shaking his head. I panicked when he fell to his knees, head in hand.

"Draggar, no," I writhed on the ground, trying to scoot my bound body over to him. "Don't listen to them! Don't listen."

Draggar lifted foggy eyes. "Marie..."

"Fight, Draggar. Don't give up. Block out their words. Only listen to mine," I spoke over the Gretolics chants.

My voice gave him the strength to focus. The cloud from his eyes cleared, and he reached for me. Our hands touched, then Draggar scooped me up into his arms, holding me close.

It was a battle of words as I verbally outmaneuvered the Gretolics commands. Draggar rose to his feet with me tucked under one arm, and his sword clutched in the opposite hand. He turned and took off at a sprint, jumping over the pile of bodies and down the tunnel.

My stomach lurched with his galloping gait. The dirt walls of the tunnel blurred past as the Gretolics voices grew farther and farther away.

I knew he would get us out of this!

Draggar jerked hard. He stumbled, dropped his sword, and threw out a hand to catch himself on the dirt wall before going down like a giant oak in the forest.

Pain lanced through my limbs, his weight a compressing force that expelled all the breath from my lungs.

"Draggar!" I nudged him with my body. He was out cold. "Draggar, wake up. Please..."

Gretolics and Valosian males began to gather around Draggar's prone form. One Valosian picked up Draggar's swords. I wanted to rip the steel from his hands.

He wasn't honorable enough to even be in Draggar's presence, much less carry the Valosian warrior's weapons.

I threw out my bound hands, clawing and pulling at the hard-packed dirt, but I couldn't scramble out from under his considerable weight. I was trapped.

"Get away from us!" I shrieked.

The Gretolic closest to me parted its thin lips, releasing a high-pitched chirping that I assumed was laughter. "You are in no position to make demands, human female."

Draggar was hoisted up at the command of the Gretolic by four Valosian males. Pride was a strange thing to feel now, but to witness it taking four males to lift my warrior made me smile inside.

A dart was plucked from Draggar's back, the culprit of what laid him out. He was merely unconscious, which meant I still had a chance to save him.

I wriggled against the male that tossed me over his shoulder. "You know, I'm really getting tired of being handled like dog food, assholes!"

"Shut her up!" a Gretolic commanded.

I gasped at the pole with the glowing blue tip. That was one of the alien items Lily found on the spaceship. She'd used it on the hand scanner that kept us trapped in our metal cages behind electrified bars. Best we could figure, the tip was electrically charged as well.

I squirmed in earnest as the male brought the glowing tip close to my face. "Touch the tip to her flesh. That should teach her how to hold her tongue until we can put her to better use."

A cold chill wrapped icy fingers around my throat. "Better use for what?"

"You won't have long to wait. Why ruin the surprise? Zap her and put her in with the others," the Gretolic commanded.

With a lifeless expression on his cold face, the Valosian male touched the glowing tip to my shoulder. An electric current flashed through me. Every muscle in my body stiffened. I couldn't move, or scream, or fight.

I just took the agony of the blinding shockwaves until my vision dimmed. The last thing I saw was Draggar's limp body being hauled ahead of mine down the tunnel where we tried to make our escape.

THE CLANGING of metal against metal jarred me awake. I remained lax as not to alert the asshole who had me slung over his shoulder that I was awake.

Draggar was being carried beside me. I could see his size eighteen boots in my periphery.

We came to a halt in the tunnel. The Gretolics were all around us. Their three-toed feet were surrounding the males who carried us. The screech of rusty hinges proceeded our forward movement.

I was being carried up a shallow ascent before the dirt tunnel gave way to a metal floor and walls. I resisted the urge to lift my head and look around. If I were going to get us out of this mess, I would need the element of surprise to do it.

Déjà vu rode me hard. I was tired of being carried around like a sack of flour. I had to bide my time. Patience and timing had gotten me away from Rayyar. I could do it again, only this time, I couldn't run away. I had to stay with Draggar.

The floor lurched and shot upwards, my stomach left behind. It was an elevator of some sort and, by the feel of it, was set to full-speed-ahead.

We came to a jolting stop. My limp body flopped, and I stole the opportunity to glance over at Draggar. With four males carrying his arms and legs, his head hung off his shoulders. His shimmering hair a silver curtain hiding his face. He breathed. And, right now, that was all that mattered.

In dire need of some WD-40, the metal door screeched open. We were carried out of the elevator and down a nondescript hallway. The floor looked clean but had been worn down to a dull pallor like it had seen many feet.

After a few feet in, the male carrying me was ordered to stop at a closed door while Draggar was carried farther down the hall. Panic choked me. I hung limp and cut my eyes hard to follow Draggar.

The males that carried him shuffled under his extreme weight and turned right at the end of the hallway. Then I lost sight of my warrior. I gulped hard and blinked away, tears blurring my vision.

The stink of Mr. Clean greeted me as I was carried inside the room. It took everything in me to remain loose. I had to follow Draggar, but first, I had to get myself free.

Element of surprise, Marie, I silently talked myself down. *Element of surprise.*

A Gretolic followed us inside. We paused at the back of the room, and I took that moment to turn my head. The sight that greeted me chilled me to the bone.

Chapter Nine

DRAGGAR

The floor beneath me looked familiar. My wrists and ankles were held tight as I floated along. I couldn't remember what happened or how I'd gotten on the prison level under the palace in the city of Huren.

Had I been injured somehow? Maybe in a war with the Nuttaki?

Then it all came crashing back. The spaceship crash-landing on the edge of the jungle. Sia Jakkar finding the human females inside. Fighting a patooga on our way back through the jungle to the settlement with the women in tow.

My long-dead ancillary heart beating back to life at the first glimpse of Marie's face. I'd never seen a being from the stars before, and I couldn't have imagined a more beautiful female.

And Rayyar had shed her blood before stealing her away from me.

My body jolted as an image of the rexose crunching down on Trisso's bones flashed like a bad dream. The feel of the tree trunk colliding with my back, a reality from my recent past.

The vision of Marie lying on the ground inside a mine shaft was what got my hearts racing. The push of adrenalyne clearing my head as nothing else could.

She'd been so brave fighting alongside me. Where was my tiny warrior now?

My head weighed more than a rynose as I tried to lift it from where it hung between my shoulders. The ends of my silvery mane trailed the floor as I was carried farther down the hall and into an interrogation room for those that had broken Valosian law.

I was intimately familiar with the layout. As a seasoned warrior, it was one of my duties to question lawbreakers before they were taken before the Royal Council for final judgment.

As I was loaded onto the rack, I never thought to be on this side of it. My arms were wrenched to the sides, and my wrists tied down with metalloid clamps, as were my ankles.

Next, I was hauled to a standing position, the weight of my limp body hanging painfully from my bound wrists.

The faces of the males under the control of the Gretolics standing off to one side were eerily blank. Had my eyes gone lifeless when the Gretolics tried to take control of my mind?

I clenched my fists, feeling my strength returning with each pump of my ancillary heart. Adrenalyne, a hormone males produced for the singular purpose of protecting a spirit mate, rushed through my veins.

Even when the first blow landed in the center of my belly, I grew stronger. I strained against my unbreakable bindings in vain as another fist cracked across my jaw.

The males took turns pummeling me. It was all for sport —the Gretolics snickering in their ear-piercing way with each hit. The males were merely obeying the commands of the Gretolics speaking into their wrist devices.

I hadn't succumbed to their mind control like the dull-eyed minions before me. Could it have been the adrenalyne that kept me from submitting completely?

A theory Nullar would need to explore and perhaps a means to defeat the Gretolics. I would need to escape first to pass along this new insight.

I tested my bonds for weaknesses. There were none, so I leaned my head back against the rack and let the four males have their fun. They were nothing more than ordinary civilians and would wear themselves out before they could do me any real damage.

Chapter Ten

MARIE

The room was filled with metal boxes stacked one atop the other. Glowing bars covered the front, imprisoning each girl housed inside.

I already knew the bars were electrified. I'd been in the same predicament after being abducted and held captive on the Gretolics spaceship that was now a smoldering heap in the jungle.

This room was larger by miles than the cargo hold on the ship, where there had only been two parallel walls of cages. In here, there were rows upon rows like in a grocery store.

There was no way of knowing how many girls were here without walking each row to look inside each cage.

The Gretolic's words haunted me. He said we were to be put to use. My heart sank over the implications. What use did they have in mind for us?

"Help me," a brunette reached out her hand as I was carried past her cage. *"Please..."*

My bottom lip trembled as I made eye contact with her. I wanted to reassure her that I would find a way to get help, but I couldn't let on that I was conscious, so I mouthed that I was sorry.

"Shut up, female." A Gretolic smacked the girl's light bars with the blue-tipped pole, showering her in a spray of stinging sparks.

Anger and empathy stirred in my gut as her doleful sob followed me. Freeing these girls would be a massive undertaking. I couldn't tell how many cages were occupied, but there had to be hundreds stacked in here.

At this point, all I had planned was to find and rescue Draggar. That in itself was daunting enough.

"That one's empty," a Gretolic rasped. "Toss her in there."

The male carrying me knelt and made to lift me off his shoulder. Now was my chance! I barely cracked open my eyelids to find only one Valosian male and two Gretolics. I was in the middle of the huge room with plenty of room to run.

I stayed limp until my butt hit cold metal. That was when I came alive. Feet planted on the Valosian's chest, I used him as a springboard and shoved myself out of his hold. I landed with a *thud*; my bare skin squeaked across the floor.

Dazed for a moment, the Valosian scrambled after me. I crab-walked away like an Olympian, flipped to my feet, and hightailed it down one row of cages and around the next.

As I rounded the corner, I ran face-first into one of the gray-faced freaks. I screamed and shoved him away. It was surprising how light the Gretolic's frail body was and how easily and how far he flew through the air before hitting the floor.

I turned and ran toward the open door. "Almost there," I chanted. "Almost there. Here I come, Draggar." The hallway was only steps away. I could taste freedom—

I slammed into the Valosian male who stepped into my path. His thick arms wrapped around me. This prick had no idea he'd just grabbed hold of a wet cat because I was a woman on a mission, and saving my warrior was priority number one.

I went batshit wild in his hold, kicking and clawing until he lost his grip and I fell to the floor. My hip took the brunt of the fall, but I felt no pain as my feet scrambled under me, and I sprinted to the back of the giant room.

At the moment, exiting out the door was a no-go. My main pursuer was the Valosian. Agile and fast, he stayed on my tail as he ran me up and down the aisles. I couldn't shake him and never could get another clear shot at the door.

The two Gretolics were useless. Their thin bodies were slow and gangly. It was shocking how they could hold up their bulbous heads on those skeletal frames.

My lungs were on fire. My thighs cramped. The fear of being locked in a metal box kept me going. I couldn't be trapped in one of those things again. I just couldn't.

But! They couldn't cage me if they couldn't find me.

I careened around the last aisle and hit the wall. The cages along the back of the room sat a foot away from it. That was my hiding spot.

Thinking thin, I slammed my back against the wall and side-stepped my ass between the wall and the cages. The Valosian tried to follow and failed. His arm stretched and waved, but I was too far away for him to grab.

"Get out, male. We'll gas her!" I heard a Gretolic screech. "Gas the entire room."

With a final look, the Valosian left the room. I heard the door click shut behind him.

The next face that appeared was the shark-toothed sneer of the Gretolic. With a gas machine in hand, he aimed it directly at me.

I slammed my eyes closed and held my breath as the noxious cloud rolled over me, filling the narrow space. Several feminine coughs echoed throughout the room. How many had been awake only to have kept quiet?

Once I rescued Draggar, I was coming back to save these girls. No way was I leaving them here.

The hiss of the gas machine seemed to go on forever. The Gretolic must have hit every cage. Just as my head went light from lack of oxygen, the hiss abruptly stopped, and the door opened and slammed shut.

I slit one eye open for a peek. Thankfully, the cloud was already beginning to dissipate. My deprived lungs protested with a heave, and I blasted out the breath I'd been holding, gagging over the fresh stink of ammonia.

Step by step, I pried my squished body out from behind the cages while keeping my breaths light and infrequent. The room beyond was obscured with the haze of the gas, so I sat with my back against the wall, listening and waiting.

There were no other sounds besides my shallow breathing. I was sure my enemy was gone, so I relaxed and took time to peer around the room.

I shook my head in disbelief over the number of aisles. It was like an alien version of Walmart, except the merchandise was abducted women.

As I was being chased, I didn't have time to do a headcount. Were Amy and Layla here? Were all the cages full or placed here in preparation for a fresh shipment? Had we been that shipment? Only we'd crashed instead?

Before the crash, I swear we were shot out of the sky, given all of the explosions. But after seeing all of this and the Gretolics at the settlement when we first arrived, it was certain Valose had been our destination all along.

The image of Jakkar and Aggar respectfully laying out the bodies of the girls that had died in the crash made me shiver. I could have been one of those girls.

For whatever reason, I survived, given a second chance. I

needed to make that second chance count. Maybe my life was meant for more on this planet.

Things on Earth hadn't exactly worked out as I'd initially planned. I lived comfortably, drove a nice car, had extra money to splurge on frivolous stuff, but what I had to do to earn that money wasn't something to brag about.

I cringed over the lie I told Lily back on the crashed ship. I told her I was an accountant. In truth, I had gone to college to pursue that field, but my career had taken a different path.

I'd desperately wanted her as a friend. I had none to speak of back home. Because of my job, I shied away from letting people get too close.

I'd been so lonely locked in that metal box with no one awake to talk to.

Lily was the first girl not to wake up screaming. After what had to have been weeks locked inside that metal box in solitude with just my thoughts for company, Lily became my friend.

She proved to be selfless and courageous, putting the lives of strangers before her own when she ventured out alone in search of help.

I needed people like her in my life. I'd grown so used to hiding what I really was that I now craved acceptance, and for once, I wanted to be looked at as someone worthy of friendship.

Maybe I should reconsider leaving Valose. I already formed a connection with Draggar, one I knew would be everlasting if I gave myself over to him. My warrior.

That was the way I thought of him, as *mine*.

On this planet, I could start over and be whoever I wanted—leave behind my dirty past and start fresh. No one would be looking for me back on Earth. Well, maybe my landlord looking for the rent, but besides that, my face wouldn't be destined for a place on a milk carton.

They reserved those spots for people like Amy and Lily. People with family and friends that would miss them. No one was going to miss me.

After my mom died, my heart became an empty husk. I longed to have a friend like Lily. To have someone care enough about me to want to watch after me. To make sure I was safe.

Draggar would be that person for me. If I let him, he would fill that void my mom had left behind.

My warrior came to my rescue after Rayyar hit me over the head and stole me away. He was part of a search party coming after Amy and Layla too, but I knew deep down that I was special to him.

I rubbed at the stirring anguish behind my sternum. That was the connection between me and Draggar wanting airtime. Did I dare turn it loose? Was I ready for a lifetime commitment that would be branded over my heart like a fleshy badge of honor?

Lily had called it a shawra. It was some sort of portal for the sharing of souls. On Valose, soulmates were a tangible thing. Crazy right?

It wasn't long before the closed door became visible. I stood on determined legs, even though my insides were swarmed with butterflies. I crept down the aisle directly in front of me, keeping my body bent low. The gas tended to float, so the air was more breathable closer to the floor.

I glanced inside the cages as I passed—some empty, some full. Me and all the girls who had been inside the cargo hold on the Gretolic's crashed ship had been meant for this room, and who knew what they had ultimately planned for us.

The door worked similarly to the ones back home with hinges and a knob of sorts. I'd wanted to find some faith, now seemed like a good time, so I said a silent prayer to Draggar's Spirits that it wasn't locked.

I turned the knob and found it tight. Panic flashed hot over my skin. Then I turned the knob in the opposite direction, and it clicked open.

"Holy shit," I whispered. "Thank you, Spirits."

Mouth dry, I stuck my head out into the hallway, looking one way and then the other. All clear, I tiptoed out and silently pulled the door closed, making the girls I was leaving behind a promise to return with help.

Sweat dotted my upper lip. They'd carried Draggar to the end of the hall and turned right, and that was where I headed. On wobbly knees, I kept close to the wall and moved quickly.

Destination reached, I paused at the junction. I looked left. There was nothing special, just more of the same dingy hallway with overhead tubular lighting and several closed doors spaced out down the length. Right was the same. Only the hallway seemed to go on forever.

Tears sprang to my eyes. Draggar could be behind any one of those doors, and I'd have to check them all to find him. My body began to shake, imagining what horrors I could accidentally run into.

I wasn't the hero type. I'd never put myself in harm's way to help another. That didn't make me a bad person. I just never had the opportunity.

Well, opportunity was knocking for this average girl from Atlanta with a shady job and wide hips.

There was no stopping the shaking in my limbs, but I did straighten my spine and took a few deep fortifying breaths. Draggar had been brave enough to rescue me, so I could put on a brave face for him—even if my lower lip trembled in fear.

I rounded the corner and stopped at the first closed door. Hand on the knob, I placed my ear to the door: nothing but a whirring of some kind of equipment. I gently turned the knob and peeked through the crack I made.

It was a dimly lit mechanical room with boxy machinery lining the walls. I closed it back and went on to the next one.

My hand on the knob, I listened and was met with more silence. I was glad not to run into anyone, but all this sneaking around made me a jittery mess.

I cracked open the door to complete darkness just as voices and heavy footfalls filtered down the hall. *Shit!* With no other options, I slipped inside the void and closed the door.

Leaning against the panel, I cringed as the voices grew closer and closer until they passed right by where I was hiding. I sagged in relief before taking a step back—

And froze as lights flooded the room.

Like a kid caught with her hand in the cookie jar, I was washed in a cold sweat and terrified to turn around to face the unknown. My eyes cut hard to the right before my head followed.

Lucky for me, it was a storage room, yet the contents left me cold. On tall shelves were clear crates of vials filled with green liquid. I was intimately familiar with the stuff. That was what the Gretolics had injected us with while they thought I was unconscious.

The liquid somehow nourished our bodies without producing any waste. I hadn't felt hungry or the need to relieve myself the entire time I lay awake while the others had remained blessedly oblivious.

I walked the length of the shelves. Maybe I could find something to use as a weapon. All I found were more green vials, the prods used to inject them, and some larger vials with blue liquid.

I discounted the row of gas machines, then paused and turned back.

The gas didn't work on the Gretolics, but I had a strong suspicion it worked on the Valosians. It was just a hunch, but why else would the Gretolic have ordered the male out of the room before he gassed me?

The gas may not knock out the Gretolics, but it could obscure their vision enough for me to get away.

I palmed one of the machines. I watched the Gretolic activate it before by squeezing the trigger on the handle. I sucked in a breath and squeezed. Noxious gas billowed out.

Breath held, I ran for the exit and listened before opening the door. With my weapon in hand, I felt a little braver as I continued my search.

The next door was locked, but I placed my ear to the panel and listened. The following two doors were the same, locked and quiet.

The muted smack of flesh meeting flesh was heard from the room across the hall. I tightened my grip on the gas machine and tiptoed over. The door was cracked open just enough for me to get a good look at a blood covered Draggar, tied up crucifixion style.

The males that had carried him from the mine shaft were taking turns punching him while two Gretolics stood off to one side. Their faces split into toothy grins like they were enjoying the show.

"Sick bastards," I grumbled.

My blood ran hot. I wanted to rush in and slap the smiles off of their gray faces, but I stayed still, white knuckling the gas machine. I needed a plan.

I ripped my eyes away from Draggar to look around as much of the room as I could see. There were four Valosian males. I could gas them, no problem.

What to do about the two Gretolics? I knew their bodies were frail, which was probably why they hid behind the Valosian's kilts using their mind control.

The glint of Draggar's swords winked at me from the

corner of the room. If I could get my hands on one of those, I could slice and dice the two gray dickheads and save Draggar.

Plan hashed, I bounced on the balls of my feet. I had one chance to pull this off. If I got caught, we'd both be screwed.

With bravado born from desperation, I shoved open the door and rushed inside. "Surprise, motherfuckers!"

Before anyone could react, I snatched up one of Draggar's swords.

"Draggar," I shouted before filling the room with gas and started swinging. "Shut your eyes and hold your breath, baby."

Chapter Eleven

DRAGGAR

At first, I thought her voice was a figment of my overactive wishful thinking. My spirit burned to be with hers. The longer I stayed tied to the rack, enduring blow after blow, the more my mind had checked out of reality.

Then the stink of something foul clouded the air. My eyes were already closed, but I complied with Marie's shout and held my breath.

The pummeling had stopped, and one after the other, bodies hit the floor with solid thumps. The screech from the Gretolics rang in my ears, but I resisted the urge to peek.

The hiss of the gaseous cloud eased, and I chanced opening my eyes to find Marie hacking her way through the two Gretolics like a true warrior of Valose.

The Spirits had truly blessed me with a female whose heart was forged from courage. She painted the walls with bright splashes of our enemy's blood which stank like death rotted over several suns-rises. Marie kept slashing at the bodies even after they ceased moving.

"Marie." Her name stuck in my dry throat. I coughed and

tried again. "Marie," I heaved out. "You can stop now, nula. They're dead. Don't waste your strength."

Marie paused mid-swing. Her head swiveled around, taking me in with rattled eyes. She held my sword aloft, bathed in the bright stink of the Gretolics. The tip dripped like a faucet onto the mangled bodies at her feet.

"They're dead," I repeated, and she nodded. "Come help me down," I coaxed.

"There were so many doors," she said with trembling lips, "I didn't know if I would find you."

"It's a good thing you got here when you did." I jokingly pulled at the metal cuffs holding me in place. "I was just about to go look for you."

Marie blinked up at me until a smirk emerged from her troubled features. "I'm sure you were just about to make your move. All joking aside, how do these cuffs come off?"

Marie knelt at my feet and tugged on the metalloid band holding my ankles to the rack.

"There's a control panel on the back side of the rack, near the top," I said. "Do you see it?"

"Yes." Marie stood on tiptoes and stretched up her arm. "What do I push?"

"The button marked 'release'."

"The writing all looks like alien hieroglyphs. What else you got?"

"The center but—" Before I could finish my sentence, Marie released me, and I crumpled to the floor. Not a good position for a male to present to his spirit mate. "Here I lay, yet I'm the one who's supposed to be saving you."

Marie tucked herself under my arm and helped me stand. "We can discuss feminism on alien worlds later. We need to get the hell out of here and find a place to lay low until we can figure a way out of this mess."

"Are you alright?"

"Me?" Marie quirked a brow. "You're the one covered in blood."

Physical injuries could be healed easier than mental ones. Marie was what we seasoned warriors called battle rattled.

I'd seen the same shaken expression on many a fledgling warrior's faces after a battle. Marie still held the gleam of fear in her eyes despite the smirk perched on her lips.

She'd shown extreme bravery in the face of great adversity. Even she was dumbfounded at the risk she took. I was happy to be free and even happier to be reunited with her, but I didn't want her to ever put her life in danger again for my benefit.

"I'll live." That was all I said.

We stepped over the bodies and retrieved my swords on the way to the door. I wiped away the blood dripping in my eyes and looked up and down the hallway. I knew exactly where we were.

"This way," I said and lurched out the door. I hated that I had to lean on her for support. A male, especially a warrior, should be able to prove they were capable of protecting their mate.

"How do you know where we are?"

"I used to live here. We're under the palace on the prison level. Back that way is the holding cells. This way is interrogation and storage rooms."

We moved fast down the hall and stopped at a closed door. My ears twitched, making slight adjustments to tease out any sounds that weren't mechanical in nature before I opened the door to the medic supply room.

"Grab that empty pack. We'll load it down with supplies."

Marie and I worked well as a team, collecting loodskins, bandages, and healing ointments. On the way out, I found protein enhancement bars given to the injured that helped speed recovery.

Then we were back out in the hall and down a hatch in the floor to a ladder that led to the maintenance tunnels. Marie had to run to keep up with my grueling pace, but I slowed after we'd put distance between us and the prison level.

I threw out a hand and sagged against the wall. I hated the weakness I presented, but now that we were relatively safe, the adrenalyne flooding my veins had worn thin. My injuries burned and throbbed. I felt every cut, every bruise.

"Let's rest here." Marie tugged on my hand.

"No," I said, measuring the pipes and tubes running overhead. "Not here. There should be a circuit room close by that runs the environmental controls inside the palace. It'll be safer there."

I found the room, punched in the code to disengage the lock, and thanked the Spirits when it clicked open. No one had thought to change the codes after the exile.

It was a small space, but I could secure the door. No one would venture down here unless there was an issue with the palace's temperature controls.

"We're safe here for now." I locked the door and slid down the wall. Marie did the same, looking me over with a critical eye. "I'm sorry I failed you. I'm not as strong as I once was in my youth."

"Are you fucking kidding me with that shit?"

The translator tucked behind my ear worked hard to decipher her words—the meanings making no sense given their usage.

"You're the toughest sonofabitch I've ever known." Marie cupped my face with her little hands. "You lost a friend to that scary-assed jungle to rescue me. No one has ever cared enough about me to go to such extremes."

"You rescued me as well." Unable to hide my flush over her words, my scales darkened to a deep blue.

"Then I guess that makes us even." Marie wiped the blood from my cheek. "Let's get you cleaned up."

Marie sifted through the supplies we found, wetting bandages with lood to clean my face. I closed my eyes, enjoying the feel of her hands fussing over me.

"Thank you for not killing the males." My spirit wept for the ones I had no choice but to dispatch in the mine shaft. "You showed mercy rendering them unconscious."

"You thank me even though they were beating the shit out of you?"

"They were innocent," I grumbled. "Only doing what those alien freaks were forcing them to do. They do not deserve to die. Not even the ones that I killed in the mine shaft deserved death. Their faces will haunt me for the rest of my suns-rises." Guilt settled around me, and I shifted on the hard floor. "I know nothing of this gas. Where did you find it?"

Marie's fingers stumbled, then paused in wiping my face. "I have so much to tell you."

I opened my eyes at her soft words. White-hot terror etched her pretty features.

"What is it?"

"We have to get help. Not just to find Amy and Layla, but to help lots of other girls," Marie gulped. "When they carried us from the mine shaft, they took me to a room with hundreds of the same metal cages just like the ones we were brought here in. Some empty, some with girls inside."

Marie scooted closer, and I brushed a strand of her dark mane away from her face. "Go on," I prompted when she froze in fear. "What else?"

"We aren't here by accident," she rushed out. "Maybe the crash was an accident—even though it felt more like we were shot down. We were meant to land on this planet. Then I found a storage room down the hall full of this green liquid the Gretolics injected us with. There are crates and crates of the stuff."

The color she spoke of was unfamiliar to me. "What is the purpose of the liquid?"

"On the ship, the Gretolics kept us knocked out with that gas." She shivered, and I drew her onto my lap. "I figured out that if I held my breath and waited, I could stay awake. Then they would come around and inject us by using a pole with a vial of that green shit attached to the end. Even after all the days I laid awake, I was never hungry or thirsty, and I never had to pee."

"So, it nourished your body somehow?"

"Yes, exactly." Marie sat stiffly, but the fear in her eyes seemed to be draining away. "Besides the shit-ton of gas machines, I also found crates of larger vials filled with a blue liquid."

My mind began to churn over what Marie had found. "Have you ever seen the blue vials before?"

"No."

The implications chilled my bones.

"We can't leave those women locked inside those cages, Draggar." Marie placed her palms on my chest, and I started to thrum for her. "We can't. Given the number of crates of vials that I saw, there are hundreds of women down there."

"And we won't." I rubbed the cold flesh of her arms. "But first, we have to get out of the palace without getting caught. I know of places we can hide inside the city until I can find a comm and contact Sia Jakkar for help."

Marie nodded and relaxed into me. She laid her head over my ancillary heart with a sigh.

"That's nice." She snuggled into me. "It's really cool how you can purr. I always liked cats."

I cocked my head as the translator stuttered over its interpretation of her foreign words. "What does it mean to perr?"

"You know, this internal vibration you're doing. I like it."

"On Valose, we call it thrumming. There are katt beings on your planet that thrum to their mates?"

"What?" Marie lifted her head and laughed. "Cat beings? Um, no. They are small animals we domesticated as pets. You know, a furry companion to love and cuddle. Don't you guys have pets on this planet?"

I shook my head over the lunacy. "I tried once, but the patooga wouldn't fit in my skypod."

"Sarcastic to the core, aren't you?"

"I learned it from you."

She scoffed at me and rolled her eyes. "So, this thrumming you're doing. Is it coming from your vocal cords?"

I slowly shook my head and took her hand to palm over my hearts. "It comes from here. It's my spirit singing to yours."

"So, you were serious about all that song from your spirit talk back in the mine shaft?" Her eyes grew wide. "That wasn't just a pickup line? You know, of you trying to seduce me out of my panties?"

"You aren't wearing any panties for me to seduce you out of."

She blinked up at me and absently rubbed her sternum.

"You feel the stirring of your spirit for mine. Can't you, tiny warrior?"

Chapter Twelve

MARIE

Tendrils of worthiness snaked their way into my heart. Draggar was singing to me, or rather, my soul. The acceptance seeping into the marrow of my cold bones was warmer than anything I'd ever felt toward any man.

Except, Draggar wasn't a man, was he. This was an alien elf dude on a foreign world.

My flimsy decision to stay here and start over had waned after what I had to do to save Draggar. Was every day going to be a life and death struggle?

And why here? Why now? Would he accept me if I told him who I really was?

I fought against the warm fuzzies I was nursing for Draggar. He swore he wouldn't mate me until I was ready. Would I ever be ready for a permanent planetary exchange?

His eyes swirled with a silver questioning, but I had no answers to give him. I didn't belong here, even if I felt like I was where I was meant to be for the first time in my life.

"I know I failed you before, but I swear I never will again. Worry not. You are safe with me, Marie," Draggar boldly stated. "I will never let anything happen to you even if it means my death. On my honor, as a warrior of Valose, of this I swear to you."

Never at a loss for words, I was struck dumb. No one had ever declared to be my protector before. Though I never trusted the word of a man, I believed him with everything in me that he would fight for me.

"Jeez, Draggar," I blushed, "you sure know how to woo a girl."

Draggar's chest rumbled with humor as he dragged me closer. I was straddling his lap, the hard ridge of his sex a hot promise of something sinfully satisfying.

Neither of us wore undergarments. It would be all too easy to pull up his kilt and impale myself on his stiff rod.

I wasn't ready for Draggar's mouth to crash over mine. We'd never kissed before, and now I was getting a taste of what I'd been missing. He explored me with his talented tongue, delving and swiping every part of my mouth.

My pussy had been privy to this, and I couldn't wait until his face was buried between my thighs once again.

He was playful as his tongue danced with mine, then demanding and almost brutal as his hands cupped my ass and swiveled my hips while he ground into me from below.

His kilt's fine fabric shielding his erection was a tantalizing friction that parted my folds, rubbing my clit in the most perfect way.

Kissed senseless, I was ready to give in and beg for something solid when Draggar's hand slipped in from behind. My pussy clenched down around the two thick fingers gliding effortlessly inside me.

My kisses turned feverish as my hips began to churn while he pumped into me from behind. My body sparked with anticipation of an impending orgasm. I ground down in search of more.

Just a shifting of material was all it would take, and I

could end my torture and impale myself on his thick cock. I could only imagine the wild ride I would be getting from all his alien extras.

Stars exploded around me, and I came on a shuddering breath. My inner muscles were spasming so tight. My release was almost painful. Draggar's cock jerked beneath me, his body going tense.

"Soon, female," he growled, punctuating his words with hard thrusts of his fingers. "I. Will. Lay. Claim. To. This. Cunt."

"Oh, fuck..." On a renewed surge of heat, I undulated on fresh waves of satisfaction. A rush of tingles coursed through my body as I wrung out every ounce of my release on his probing fingers.

I trembled as he gently withdrew—not from his touch, but from how close I'd been to casting aside my inhibitions and taking his cock out for a test drive. There was no denying I craved what he was packing. His erotic anatomy was what wet dreams were made of.

One taste of that craving would bind me to him forever—body and soul. I could feel myself reaching for the lifeline he was extending. If I weakened... if I took it, the home I knew would be lost to me forever.

He cleaned me up and then himself. I settled on his lap in his loose embrace while we shared a meal of crumbly protein bars and lood, the Valose equivalent to water.

With both my appetites sated, Draggar reclined back and tucked my head under his chin. I'd never felt cared for in my life until now. It was a strange and comforting feeling to be treasured.

I nuzzled his chest and moaned at his spicy scent. "What makes you so irresistible?"

"My bubbly personality."

His answer was so deadpan. I had to slap a hand across my

mouth to suppress my burst of laughter. Draggar was so much like me in so many ways. We shared pain. Maybe not for the same reasons, but we both bore bruises on our souls.

Draggar's mouth touched mine in a long, reverent kiss before arranging my limbs and placing his cheek on the top of my head.

Mine! Something deep inside me screamed. This warrior was mine.

I drifted off to sleep with a knowing smile on my lips that I was totally fucked.

Chapter Thirteen

DRAGGAR

My spirit mate slept so sweetly that I debated on waking her. The urgency to get moving wouldn't rest. I had no way of knowing if the suns had risen or fallen.

I'd found Marie at the top of the suns-rise, but my body healed as if many hurs passed. I could only guess at how long we'd been on our own.

Though I remained awake and detected no other sounds than the machines working around us, the Gretolics would be searching the palace for us, and it was only a matter of time before they made their way down here.

We needed a better place to hide. Though the warrior in me grated against hiding, common sense told me I couldn't fight them all. Pride came second to keeping my spirit mate safe.

"Tiny warrior." Cradled in my arms, I spoke softly and gently jostled her. She stirred but didn't wake. "Nula, we must go." She sighed and turned her face into my chest. The heat from her breath washed over my scales in a riot of blues and whites.

Oh my hearts, this female had to give in to the pull of her

spirit soon. I ached to join with her, not just in body but in mind. I yearned to feel her presence within me.

It'd been so long since I last felt the echo of another's spirit. As I peered down into her lovely features, I could no sooner compare what I'd felt for Nakkia than I could for Marie. I knew once we mated, the intensity of the bond would be just as fierce.

Bonding with two females in a single lifetime? Who would have imagined it? Not I. Then again, finding a second spirit mate couldn't have come at a more dangerous time. The gravity of my thoughts turned my blood cold.

"Marie." My voice turned harsh.

Her eyes flew open. "What's happened? Are we caught?"

"No." I swallowed and tried to temper the urge to flee. "But we need to move before we're found."

Marie nodded, and my tiny warrior sprang to her feet. "Then let's blaze a trail."

I cocked my head. "Does setting the path you travel on fire help hide your tracks on your world?"

"What?" she snickered. "No. It's a figure of speech. You know, like slang words."

I shook my head. "Your culture is very different than mine."

"It sure as fuck is," she mumbled, gathering what little we carried with us.

I holstered my swords, shouldered the pack she handed me, and placed my ear to the door. No sounds came from the maintenance tunnel. I disengaged the lock and cracked open the door just enough for a peek.

I stepped out and motioned for Marie to stay inside until I cleared the tunnel. Then I curled my fingers for her to follow. We crept the remaining length of the tunnel until we reached a junction.

Right would take us to another lift that would lead to

the upper levels of the palace. Left would take us down another level to the air exchangers. That was where we were going.

Marie clung to my arm as we descended the steep stairwell. I led her around at the base of the steps and through a door leading to the main air intake duct.

I silently closed the door and engaged the lock.

Marie whispered with wide eyes, "What is this place?"

"An air duct that will lead us out of the palace," I whispered back.

"That's the biggest fan I've ever seen," she waved her hand at the circulator behind us. "That thing is like a wind tunnel from hell."

Just then, the circulator kicked on. Marie yelped as fresh air pulled her toward the warrior-sized blades. I planted my boots against the roaring air current and swung Marie into my arms. She stiffened before tucking her body in close to mine.

There was no talking above the flow of air. My nod and her smile were all that were exchanged as I held my precious bundle tight and fought against the rush of air pushing against my body.

Head down and body aimed into the current. It was a slow forward progression. With every step, the soles of my boots slid backward on the slick metal floor of the duct.

I kept sure-footed, making sure I had one foot firmly planted before raising the other as we sluggishly crept toward freedom.

The abrupt halt of the air circulator nearly sent me toppling head over heels. With the rush of air now ceased, I ran the remainder of the way to the grate leading to the outside.

There was no other way out than through here. I needed to remove the barrier and get us out before the circulator kicked back on. I couldn't hold Marie and tear the grate off its welded frame.

"Crouch low and wrap your arms around my leg," I instructed as I set Marie on her feet. "If the circulator kicks back on, hold on tight, or you'll be sucked back through the ducting."

"Okay," she panted. "Okay, hold on for dear life. Got it. No making sushi out of Marie."

Her hold was strong, but her body trembled as she did what I asked. With both hands, I gripped one side of the grate and pulled.

At first, nothing budged, then the blessed creak of metal bars giving way under pressure echoed through the duct.

"Fucking Helios!" I cursed at the noise. "You'd have to be deaf not to have heard that."

I reached down deep, willing my ancillary heart to pump more adrenalyne. Fiery power flooded my veins, giving me the strength of three warriors. Through gritted teeth, I easily peeled back the grate.

I stuck my head out through the hole and peered down at the ten fates drop before grabbing Marie. She sucked back a harsh breath as we dropped to the rocky ledge below.

Marie stumbled when I set her on her feet, then fell back on her ass at her first glimpse of the churning waters of the Caspeen Sea. "We, um... We aren't *ppplanning* to cliff dive off here into that, are we, Draggar?"

I scoffed, "Helios, no! Even if we survived the fall, the chances of not being eaten by the squidlin are nil. Besides, we are trapped inside the dome shielding around the city."

"How have you people managed to thrive and prosper on this death trap?" she groused. I pulled her up by the hand she held out to me. "You live inside Jurassic Park, the plants want to eat you, and there's death lying in wait beneath the waters bordering your city."

"By the tips of our swords," I unsheathed one of my swords and poked at the dome. The transparent shield rippled in a shimmer around the tip, "and most recently, this impenetrable dome. But I wouldn't call the extinction of our females thriving," I snorted. "After what we encountered in the mines and what you described in the storage rooms, our prosperity may soon be coming to an end."

"I'm so sorry, Draggar. It comes naturally for me to be a raging bitch. That was a nasty thing for me to say." Marie dropped her eyes. "I can't imagine what Earth would be like under an alien invasion."

Shame gutted me of anger. "Forgive me, nula. I shouldn't have snapped at you." None of this was her fault.

"That's okay. I don't blame you for being pissed off." Marie squeezed my hand. "Now that we're out of that mess, we need to get to the settlement and bring back reinforcements to free all those women. I wish I knew for sure if Amy was in there with them. And Layla, too. Even though she is a spoiled brat."

I growled, envisioning a war against the Gretolics. "Freeing the women will be the first mission, but we aren't going back to the settlement."

"Why not? What happened? Where are we going?"

I sheathed my sword and took her hand, leading the way off the ledge as she hit me with rapid-fire questions. "After you and the others came up missing, we found Gretolic tracks as well as our own people's where a rynose pod had breached the wall. The beasts had been herded to destroy the wall purposely. Sia Jakkar is moving everyone to the Caverns of the Ancients."

"But why? Can't you just repair the wall?"

"The Gretolics are using our own people against us. Enough talk." I glanced back, growing more agitated the longer we stood here. I motioned for Marie to climb the rocky incline ahead of me. "Ascend, female." I motioned for Marie to climb the cliff's steps ahead of me.

"Are you sure this is safe?" She gulped and looked down at the sheer drop into the dark waves hitting the base of the cliff.

"Keep close to the wall and don't look down."

"That doesn't inspire confidence."

"That's why I'll be climbing up behind. In case you get dizzy, I can grab hold of you before you plummet to your death."

"How gallant of you." Marie nervously swatted at my chest. "And here I thought it was because you were trying to look up my dress."

Lust erupted into a firestorm, burning me from the inside out. I snagged her around the waist and brought her up against my body.

"It's true this garment offends me." I buried my face in the hollow of her throat. Her intoxicating scent swayed me on my feet. "It should be made Valose law that a body so perfect not be covered."

"Jesus Christ, Draggar," she hissed. "Words should not make a girl this wet. My very own silver seducer is determined to have his way with me."

"If our lives weren't in jeopardy, I would strip you of this dress and plunge my cock into your hot sheath." The scent of her arousal flashed over my scales in a silvery riot. "But first, I would have your taste fresh on my tongue while I fucked you."

"Holy shit!" Marie moaned and undulated against me.

She was a tempting morsel, but as much as I wanted her on my tongue, I wouldn't risk her safety for a few mims of pleasure. My warrior instincts told me we were being hunted.

The trail I'd left in the form of the damaged grate would

be discovered sooner or later. We were easy pickings out on this ledge with no place to run.

"Here's the thing about teasing." I pulled her against the length of my body and ground my erection into her soft belly. I relished the glaze of need veiling her eyes. "Two can play at this game."

"You play dirty, Draggar."

"When you consent and let me inside your sweet cunt, I promise to play even dirtier," I growled.

Chapter Fourteen

MARIE

Draggar's dirty pep talk got me moving up the rocky steps carved out of the side of the cliff. My fear of heights left behind with the promise of him finding us a hiding place where he would—and I quote—*devour my cunt until I begged him to stop*.

We were in a life and death situation, then again, ever since I crash-landed on this silver planet, when had I not been?

So, I thought it fitting, after all the scary shit I had managed to live through, to adopt a new motto. *Take pleasure whenever I could and as much of it as I could get.* And Draggar was more than willing to make that happen.

He liked to eat pussy, so who was I to deny him that pleasure.

When he pressed me against the ridge of his erection, my belly tightened with a lick of heat. It seemed the longer I denied him, the more and more I craved to have him inside me.

There was more to this yearning than lust. Something wild culminated under my bones. Something hot and feral. It stirred and pressed against my sternum, aching to be let loose.

It was a burning need I couldn't explain. It went beyond sex. Beyond the lifeline of safety Draggar extended.

The whole of my being wanted him. I wasn't sure how much longer I could hold back this overpowering desire to become one with him.

I suppressed the urge to kiss the ground when we finished our climb. I stuck to Draggar like glue as we ducked behind a large rectangular structure and glanced back in the direction we came from. I nearly fell over.

Like a giant crystal rising from the ground, the palace threatened to touch the clouds. The walls of the imposing skyscraper sparkled in the twin suns that warmed us from above. It was a multifaceted jewel set among smaller white buildings surrounding its base.

In the center of the city sat a circular fountain worthy of the wealthiest Las Vegas casino. Streams of sparkling water shot high into the air.

"Atlantis," I murmured. That's what the city of Huren looked like. At least what I imagined the lost city of Atlantis looked like. It was a damn shame I didn't have a camera. I'd love to show all the girls once we joined them at the caverns.

I turned back to find Draggar's head cocked to one side. His pointed ears twitched and swiveled as he listened to something beyond my auditory capacity.

He made a motion of talking with his hand and pointed to the wall of the structure behind where we were crouched.

He waved me forward. We kept low, and I followed him to a vent embedded in the wall. We peered through the slats and—

Holyfuckingshit! Parked inside was an alien spacecraft. Black as sin, the hull was shiny yet reflected none of the Valosian's milling around it.

Panels had been removed from various areas around the outside to reveal the inner workings. They appeared to be repairing it. Off to one side sat a smaller, not as impressive example of spacecraft.

It looked like it was being dismantled. Parts and pieces of the craft were strewn all around the floor like it spewed its guts, and the Gretolics were picking through the aftermath.

I shot a look at Draggar beside me. His face was set in a grim mask, and the air around him felt chilled. Something about the scene before us was definitely wrong.

We crept to the end of the building. I hung back while Draggar peered around the corner. He gave the signal to follow, and I was on his ass like white on rice as we made a run for a small circular structure.

Once inside, I couldn't control my trembling. Fear had taken hold of me, and I found it hard to breathe. Now was not a good time for a panic attack, so I took deep breaths to calm myself.

The interior of the structure smelled earthy and slightly of leather. It was dark except for a shaft of light cutting through the darkness.

Draggar kept low, moving through the dark interior with ease. I stumbled along behind him, following his skin markings' glowing patterns until we reached the source of the light coming from a narrow window.

He sucked back a gasp, and I scrambled up beside him to see what had brought about his reaction.

Having come in through the back door, we faced the city's interior. The fountain was glorious and beckoned me to splash in its shimmering waves, but there was no taking my eyes off the palace. All smooth wall for the first fifty feet, then it turned jagged, terraced off at irregular intervals.

"So pretty," I whispered.

"So empty," Draggar returned.

"How can you tell it's empty?"

"Not the palace, the city." Draggar dropped to his ass with his back against the wall. "The streets are empty. Where has everyone gone? There's no one."

"Maybe they're all inside." I dragged my eyes away from the palace and sat down beside him. "How many people are normally out and about this time of day?"

"During the suns-rise, the streets are usually bustling with males."

I rose to peer out the window once more. Now that I wasn't mesmerized by the palace's beauty, I took note of the empty streets. A variety of tools and strange conveyances littered the landscape as if everyone had suddenly dropped what they were doing and—just left.

The eerie quiet made the hair on the back of my neck stand at attention.

"Where are we anyway?" I gestured around the small space.

"A tanning hut." Draggar lifted the edge of a fur stacked nearby. "By the looks of the place, no one has been working here in a long while."

Draggar kicked at a stack of furs with a curse. He flopped against the wall at his back—head in hand—digging his fingers into his hair and pulling at his scalp.

I empathized with his frustration. He on his world and me lost to mine, yet we were both victims of the Gretolics. I scooted in close and laid my hand on top of his silky head.

"Don't tear out your beautiful hair," I soothed.

His hands fell away, clearly deflated. I tunneled my fingers through his silky strands as he wrapped his arms around my waist.

"Are we safe here?"

"There is no safe place on Valose," he gritted out.

That was not the answer I expected to hear from my

fierce warrior. "We have to get out of here, Draggar. Please don't give up."

"I will never give up on you." He sat forward so fast. I jerked back. The intensity with which he spoke was startling. "I've lost one spirit mate. I will not lose another. I just need a moment to absorb all of what is happening."

I swallowed hard, wondering how he would take it if I found a spacecraft to return me to Earth along with the other girls. According to Lily, sex was what sealed the deal, and that was when the matching shawras materialized. So, technically, we weren't spirit mates.

Yet.

"First, we need a comm to contact Zikkar. Getting out of the dome is nearly impossible. I know there have been recent power fluctuations. If I could ping Zikkar, maybe he could find a weakness in the shielding for us to escape through."

"Okay, good." I sat up straighter. "Where would we find a comm?"

"Maybe Zikkar's old cottage. Or perhaps his educator, Hexxus. If anyone has extra technology lying around, it would be one of them. But their cottages are located on the other side of the city."

"And how do we get over there without being caught?"

"I'm not sure that we can." He looked at me steadily. "The city I once knew no longer exists. The enemy seems to be everywhere."

"I thought there was a gate to get out of here."

"The control room is in the center of the palace. Even if we could gain access to the gate's controls, one of us would have to stay behind to keep it open for the other to escape."

"Wait!" I popped up on my knees. "You said *nearly impossible*, so there's another way."

He looked at me steadily. "The only way out of the dome aside from the gate is under it."

"So, we dig a tunnel—"

"Impossible. There are sensors all around the shielding that detect ground tremors."

I threw my hands up. "I give up. First, you imply there's a way, and then you cockblock it with ground sensors. So, is there or isn't there—"

"It's through the recirculating pipes that carry fresh lood to and from the fountain."

"What are we waiting for? Let's do that."

"The pipes stretch for a hundredth fates before emptying in the Twien River."

I just sat staring at him and waited for the deadly punchline. Nothing had ever been easy since crash-landing on Valose, and I didn't expect escaping from the city to be either.

"The river skirts the edge of a floratrap field, so even if you could hold your breath long enough, the carnivorous plants could possibly devour us once we emerge."

In my mind, drums and cymbals beat out the rimshot comedy sound effect, ba-dum-tis. Except there was nothing funny about any of this.

Draggar rose from the floor, navigating through the darkness like a cat. His hulking frame a darker blob that I followed with my eyes.

He returned with an armload of furs and spread them out on the floor. It was an inopportune time for my lady parts to tingle, but he had promised to eat me until I begged for mercy.

After he spread out the furs creating a makeshift bed, he sat back on his haunches and curled his fingers at me.

"Yes, sir." I happily hurried over, but when all he did was settle me on the pallet and cover me with a fur, my smile of anticipation fell away.

"Rest while you can," he said. "I need to observe the

movements of the city before we can move again."

"I guess a tongue lashing isn't in my future, huh?" I was only half teasing. I could go for a distraction—Draggar style —right about now.

His sculpted lip curled back in a sexy sneer. "Not to worry, tiny warrior. Once we're in a safer location, I have plans for you."

Chapter Fifteen

DRAGGAR

I didn't know what I expected. The emptiness of a once vibrant city wasn't it. We suspected the Gretolics had taken control, but this was far worse than what I'd imagined.

Our gray enemy had a serious foothold in Huren, maybe even the planet.

Where were all the civilians that should have been going about their tasks? Where were all the younglings and nurslings that should be playing in the park? Not even a stray warrior roamed the streets.

The only activity had been in the mines and Sia Sakkar's spacecraft hanger.

Both weighed heavily on me. So much so, it curbed my appetite for the taste of my mate, which seemed impossible.

Valosians were accustomed to living with uncertainty. Our world was a dangerous place, but we lived our lives and accepted fear as a part of it. But this... This was different. I had no idea how to fight this new enemy.

Sia Jakkar had been planning a recon mission before the rynose pod attack on the settlement, and I volunteered to be part of it. As a warrior of Valose, I had to do my due diligence to learn everything I could while I found a way to get Marie out of here.

My warrior instincts roared within me. I was in the perfect position to gather as much information about what was taking place inside the city as I could before we made our exit.

I scanned the grounds before my eyes landed on the hanger. Sia Sakkar's craft was being dismantled, scavenged for parts. I had to guess the Gretolics were repairing their much larger ship.

I prayed to the Spirits they were only here to repair their vessel and vacate. Yet, what were they planning to take with them on their way off-planet?

Why were they so interested in mining for nutrillium that they had used dampeners to hide the noise of the excavators? Was our mineral a source of power for them too?

What of the storage room full of caged females? What was their destiny?

I swallowed hard over the empty city streets and the storage room full of blue vials Marie had found. Were my people caged somewhere like the females? The vials their source of nutrition?

So many questions bounced around inside my skull. I hated not understanding my enemy. My palms itched to unsheathe my swords and cut down every Gretolic I laid eyes on, but the reason for my second heartbeat stirred restlessly on the pallet beside me.

I longed to join her. To fulfill my promise of pleasuring her. I would, but not here. She was too great of a distraction, and I needed all my senses at full capacity to keep her safe.

I observed the city until the twin suns touched the horizon, and Marie's deep, even breathing filled the hut.

I swallowed past my dry throat. I'd seen nothing so far. No movement of any kind. Not even the semblance of a search party coming to look for us. It was as if the city died.

An uneasy chill settled around me.

A lone wetlock soared overhead. Its leathery wings stretched taut, catching the sultry jungle breeze blocked by the dome. With deadly claws extended, it swooped down and scratched at the translucent shielding before flying away.

The screech of the warrior-sized door on the hanger ripped through the silence of the city. My scales flashed in warning as a group of Gretolics followed behind a line of Valosian males.

I recognized the males from the maintenance team Sia Sakkar had assembled to maintain his spacecraft. Eyes forward, they walked as if under a spell, no conversation being exchanged or joking around with shoulder punches.

They were taken to an access door that led to the depository where nutrillium was stockpiled for Sia Sakkar's spacecraft. The males were ushered inside. One of the Gretolics spoke into its wrist device before shutting the door and locking the males inside.

"What in the Spirits are those gray fuckers up to?" I murmured.

Not long after, movement on the opposite side of the city caught my eye. Up high, I squinted into the waning suns' light. An odd conveyance flew closer before gently descending to the ground. It was oval in shape but hollowed out for seating two wide.

It was like nothing I'd ever seen before. Unlike our rovers, which could only float a few fates above the ground, the conveyance the Gretolic was operating could take to the sky.

A male exited on the passenger side. His face one that I hadn't seen since I joined Sia Jakkar in his exile munthis ago.

"Hexxus," I breathed into the quiet of the tanning hut. "What are they doing with you?"

He didn't appear to be under their mind control. The male moved as if he retained all his faculties. When the Gretolics approached him, I lifted and swiveled my ears forward, straining to pick up on their conversation.

They spoke of transmitters and comm technology that made little sense to my warrior training. I knew of weapons and fighting, not about the inner workings of technological devices.

What I did understand was how Hexxus appeared to be working with the Gretolics, uncoerced.

A rumbling growl boiled deep in my chest as my eyes narrowed on the traitor. Considered the most brilliant mind amid all the males of Clan Huren, he had ushered in all our advancements.

We went from living in stone structures with wooden walls to keep out the jungle, to an impenetrable dome powered by the reconfiguration of depleted nutrone spears the Nuttaki had left behind.

Hexxus had created gravity disruptors that were responsible for the operation of our skypods and rovers. He'd even designed and built a spacecraft for Sia Sakkar that could touch the stars.

From one suns-rise to the next, Clan Huren rose to a technological power far beyond the other two clans. No questions had ever been asked as to how he did it. We simply accepted his discoveries without question.

Something snapped inside my mind. A puzzle piece dropped into place. Had Hexxus sold us out in exchange for knowledge from these gray freaks?

What of Zikkar? His closest pupil? Was he in on this too? Was Sia Jakkar moving the settlement to the Caverns of the Ancients with a spy in tow?

I needed to get my hands on a comm and soon. Sia Jakkar needed to be warned.

The conversation across the field came to an end. Hexxus followed a Gretolic into the hanger while the others dispersed, taking the flying conveyance with them.

I bided my time until the moon took its place in the dark sky. I nudged Marie awake. She sat up, rubbing at her eyes.

"We need to move now."

"Where?"

"To the warrior training grounds on the eastern side of the city," I explained, adding a few rolled furs to our pack of supplies. "Only the warriors that joined Sia Jakkar in his exile ever used it after the dome was built. With the city desolate, I suspect we'll find it empty."

"Then, let's go." Marie stood and straightened her filthy dress. "I wished I'd changed back into my clothes that Lily found, but they reminded me too much of how I got to this freakshow of a planet. No offense." She held up her hands and grinned. "Anything would be better than this nasty Gretolic couture."

I found a basket of soft pelts. Sifting through the pile, I picked out a couple of the largest furs. "If I had an extra kiltus, I would give it to you to wear." I handed her the furs. "These aren't fabric, but they're supple and workable. Perhaps you can fashion yourself a dress once we reach the training grounds."

"Ohmygod." Marie rubbed the furs against her cheek. "These are so luxurious. Thanks."

I was anxious to get moving, but I took a moment to watch my spirit mate enjoy something I provided. "We stay low and stick close to the dome's perimeter. No talking. You must stay close to me. Move when I move and run when I run."

"Yes, master." She gave me a cheeky grin.

"It is imperative you follow my lead. Huren is swarming with Gretolics."

"I know." Marie visibly deflated. "All kidding aside. I promise to do as I'm told. I'm just so tired of being in danger. All I want is a bath, clean clothes, and a bottle of wine."

I bowed my head and held open my arms. She fell into me, and I gathered her close. "I don't know what the equivalent of why-ne is on Valose, but I promise, once we are out of Huren and back with the others, I will do everything in my power to get you whatever you desire."

Chapter Sixteen

MARIE

It took everything in me to follow Draggar out of the tanning hut. The city was deceptively deserted. The illusion of safety inside the hut from all the quiet made me want to stay and get cozy with Draggar.

He insisted we wouldn't remain safe where we were, so off we went into the night. Me being five-foot-two—and that was standing up straight—Draggar's stride far exceeded mine. For every one of his steps, I had to take three, yet I somehow kept up.

We'd been running for days. My lungs burned almost as much as my thighs. Just when I thought I couldn't go another step, Draggar stopped dead in his tracks.

It was like hitting a brick wall when I bounced off his backside. I landed on the ground with a hard ump.

Draggar whipped around and pulled me to him. We crouched as one, with Draggar's hand covering my mouth. To my credit, I made no other sounds despite my sore rear-end.

I didn't see it at first until I followed the direction of Draggar's intense gaze. I squinted hard into the darkness until I could just make out the oval silhouette of an approaching vessel descending from the night sky.

The Gretolic flying—what reminded me of a deviled egg —landed without so much as a whisper next to a row of the same crafts lined up in a large field.

Draggar went tense around me. Without taking his eyes off the Gretolic, he nudged me behind him and, with great care, soundlessly unsheathed his twin swords.

The alien exited, then paused. With its beady eyes set too close together inside its bulbous head, it looked in our direction and then all around as if it sensed something was wrong.

Uneasiness rolled off Draggar in waves. He was crouched, ready to launch himself at the Gretolic if it so much as looked like it was going to head our way.

With a last look around, the alien turned and moved off in the opposite direction. Draggar's broad shoulders dropped. The muscles of his back eased.

I'd been frozen in fear. Now every ounce of tension leached out of my body, and I slumped to the cool blue dirt. Left in its wake was overwhelming exhaustion.

I really needed a vacation. I was so fucking sick of being afraid.

Draggar motioned for me to follow him to a small building off to the side of the field. We made a run for it and paused with our backs against the stone wall before slipping inside.

The interior was pitch black, so I tucked my fingers into the waistband of Draggar's kilt as he navigated us through to a door in the far back. Once inside, he shut us in together. The clunk of a lock engaging echoed around the space.

"We'll be safe in here," Draggar spoke for the first time since we left the tanning hut. "This is Sia Jakkar's personal space at the training grounds. There's an escape hatch under the bed that only a few of us have knowledge of."

"There's a real bed in here?" I immediately locked on to the mention of the unexpected luxury. "I can't remember the last time I slept in a bed."

I couldn't see my hand in front of my face, but that didn't stop me from moving around the space. My shin made contact with something hard, and Draggar came to my rescue, swooping me up into his impossibly strong arms and carrying me over to the bed.

My body sunk into the pillowy softness. "Thank you, oh gallant one." I giggled, thrilled to feel something familiar, even if I couldn't see it.

Draggar grunted and moved away. The loss of his body left me aching for his heat in more than one place.

I wasn't sure what set off the tingles between my thighs— whether it was from relief of the relative safety or naughty thoughts of how Draggar and I could make use of this bed.

A soft glow from one of those weird glow-in-the-dark rocks set the room in dim light. It was enough so I could see the sparse furnishings around me. And the cut of Draggar's powerful body.

"I can smell your arousal, female," Draggar accused.

"Sorry. Not sorry." I shot him a devious grin. "Wasn't there some talk about devouring my cunt?" I never used the "c" word, but it now seemed appropriate, and something about speaking the word out loud speared sparks of desire directly to my core. I lifted my knees and let my legs fall open. "Here's your blatant invitation, or were you just talking smack?"

Draggar descending on me with a roar. *Fuck!* I hope the Gretolics hadn't heard that—

All thought left me with the lashing of his tongue across my clit. Two fingers joined the assault, and all too soon, I was crashing on a wave of sharp, rich pleasure.

His fingers played in my juices while he suckled my clit. I

writhed under the leisurely onslaught until Draggar upped his game and speared me with his thick tongue. My back arched off the bed, and I was gifted with the vibrations he called thrumming.

He was like a living, breathing dildo, fucking me with his vibrating tongue. When he brought me to orgasm for the second time, I choked on my screams.

Draggar rose above me, dragging my body down to the foot of the bed to straddle his tight waist. I lay on my back with him sitting back on his knees.

He palmed my pelvis and ground into me. I moved with the motion of his hips, relishing the hard ridge pushing against my sensitive bits.

All it would take to have him inside me was a simple lift of his kilt. His cock was right there for the taking, and he wouldn't object if I feed his length inside me.

A rush of wetness added to my heat. The stirring behind my breastbone grew agitated and frantic. I was swept up in a fierce lust that took my body by storm. I needed to squelch this rising tide before I drowned in my own desires.

As if Draggar could read my mind, I was divested of my dress that had bunched up around my hips. Gloriously naked, I stretched under his languid perusal.

Hunger swirled in the silver of his gaze. And I was just as ravenous.

"Get naked!" I demanded. "I want to see all of you."

Draggar left me so fast, I yelped. He shucked his boots and kilt, forgetting his empty sword harness still crossed over his back, and dove on top of me.

His cock jutted out between us. The bulbous head spewing a thick fluid as I took him in hand. I loved the way his alien cock felt against my palm. All the bumps and ridges, erotic candy for my flesh.

"I would sample these," he growled.

With a strangled cry, he pulled first one nipple and then the other into the heat of his mouth. He swirled his talented tongue around my pebbled peaks until I was a writhing mess beneath him.

"And I would sample this." I squeezed his cock before lining the head of him up with my slick core. "Fuck me, Draggar. Make me yours."

There was no changing my mind. I was too far gone. The need to be fucked, to be claimed by this male, went beyond any rational thought.

He entered me slowly, stretching me by degrees as he fed his enormous cock inside me. Every bump, every ridge, was a treat for my starved pussy.

His face a fierce mask of possessiveness that sent my heart pounding. So focused on holding himself in check, one fang had punctured his lower lip. A drop of his blue blood threatened to spill.

I couldn't recall the last time I'd gotten laid. With Draggar, and every inch he pushed inside me, evaporated all other memories of those few that came before him.

I trembled and whimpered from the fullness. Afraid, yet eager to know the feel of him. I was a born-again virgin taking an alien cock for the first time.

Wanting a better view, I lifted onto my elbows to gaze down at where we were joined. I was right. All those alien extras were making my pussy sing, bumping along my clit as he took his time entering me.

I breathed through the onslaught. I was full to the gills when he seated himself fully. Impaled with his massive cock, my pussy was stretched so tight, it was unrecognizable.

"Mine," he uttered through bared teeth before pulling out to slowly push back inside.

His cock coated in my juices, I watched with stunted breath as he sheathed himself again, my pussy spreading to accommodate his girth.

The triangular-shaped flaps at the base of his cock came out to play on his third stroke, and I nearly flew out of my skin when they teased my clit.

I watched him fuck me slow and steady, moaning and uttering deliriously through the onslaught of sensation. Every nub and ridge of his cock was made for a woman's pleasure.

I swiveled my hips in time with his languid thrusts until all the dangers of this world fell away, and all I knew was him. The pleasure. The scent of our coupling.

I fell back from the decadence of being fucked by my warrior. Draggar followed, falling forward on his hands, planting them on either side of my head.

He leaned down to claim my mouth with deliberate thrusts of his tongue. I dug my fingernails into the scales on his back, arching up to meet his muscled chest as he buried himself inside me.

And that was when it happened.

I came on a wave of desire so strong, it pulled me under. Warmth and light spread through every cell of my being before a raging swirl hit me between my breasts.

Something hot and amorous filled my heart. For the first time in my life, I felt like I was whole. A puzzle with one missing piece was finally complete.

Draggar took my hands in his and worshipped me with his cock. He'd been slow at first. Now he was wild, feral in the taking of me. It was no longer just my pleasure I felt, but the echo of his.

I fed off the sensation and let myself go completely. Another orgasm swelled and erupted. I arched, riding out the tidal waves.

Draggar was in complete control as I clung to his shoulders. He took me so thoroughly, so completely, when he swelled and exploded inside of me, there was no doubt to whom I belonged.

Chapter Seventeen

DRAGGAR

It should be made into Valosian law not to disturb a newly bonded couple on the first suns-rise after their mating. I nuzzled the back of Marie's neck and squeezed the breast filling my palm.

Like the insatiable spirit mate she proved to be throughout the suns-fall, Marie moaned and wiggled her backside into my stiffening cock. She had a sex drive that matched my own.

I grumbled and rolled her onto her belly, lining the head of my cock up with her eager slit. She arched her back in an invitation for me to plunge in deep—

Then reality slapped me in the face.

We weren't at the settlement in my skypod about to enjoy a suns-rise of bed play. We were hiding in the back room of the weapons cottage Sia Jakkar used as his personal space. Lust had dampened my warrior instincts, and I allowed the enemy to walk up on us—unsuspected.

The rummaging sound came again. A deep voice mumbled, and footsteps shuffled closer. The rattle of the doorknob set us both on alert. The echo of Marie's spirit, a smoldering fire of promise, recoiled in fear.

Rolling from the bed in a lithe move, I gestured for Marie to get up and dress. Her movements were fast and jerky as her spirit shivered within me.

I slung my discarded kiltus around my hips and palmed my swords. With Marie behind me, I tapped the hidden lever to raise the bed and revealed the hatch.

Marie needed no direction as she hurried over and crawled into the dark tunnel Aggar and I had carved out of the earth as an escape exit for our Sia.

We never expected to use it, but something about our new City of Huren never felt entirely right to the seasoned warriors who had, ultimately, followed Sia Jakkar.

I went in after her and pulled the hatch shut. We were left in total darkness, and I cursed the rumpled bedding above us. The scent of our mating perfumed the air. You'd have to be a damn fool not to know the room had recently been occupied.

It was only a moment before the lock on the door unscrambled from where I jammed it. Only someone proficient in technology could work that fast, and I knew the name of our visitor without a doubt.

Hexxus.

I glanced back at a wide-eyed Marie. I'd promised her safety, even at my own expense, and I would fulfill that promise. If Hexxus came alone, now might be the only chance to gather inside information.

The interrogator in me needed to get to the bottom of why he felt the need to betray his own people.

My spirit mate gave me a stiff nod. With our spirits entangled, she could feel my request without a single word being spoken.

I refused to put her in any danger, so I peeked through

the slit in the hatch. Hexxus was alone and approaching the bed with a curious look on his face.

Before he could guess at what happened, I sprang from the hatch, knocking him on his ass. Swords drawn and ready to cleave him in two, Hexxus flashed his palms in surrender.

"How... *How* did you get inside the dome?" Hexxus' s lips quivered out the words.

I wasn't about to tell him of Marie's accidental drop into a mine shaft dug too close to the surface. Or about Marie at all, for that matter. "You weren't aware your new friends brought me here?"

"I thought you'd left when Sia Jakkar was exiled." Hexxus scratched his frazzled head.

"Care to explain why you sold out your own people?" Hexxus jerked back as the tip of my sword touched the soft flesh under his chin.

"I hadn't meant it to go this far," Hexxus rattled out. "It was only supposed to be an exchange of knowledge for the nutrillium they needed to power their craft, and then they were to be on their way."

"Narcissistic prick! You conspired with aliens to feed your ego."

"No. No. It hadn't begun that way. I only wanted to create the dome to protect the city. Nothing more. Now, everything is out of control. You don't understand, Draggar," Hexxus rushed out, "I'm not working with the Gretolics."

"No?" I sneered in disbelief. "Then why are you the only male in Huren not under their mind control?"

"Because they need what's inside my head, and they can't get it if I'm under their control."

"What could you possibly have knowledge of that a being capable of navigating the stars would need?" I lifted his chin with the tip of my sword.

"It would put you in danger if I were to tell you..." Hexxus' words faded off as he stared through me.

"You're lying." I pressed the tip of my sword to the main artery frantically pulsing in his neck to regain his attention. "You know nothing. And the Gretolics knew where and how to hit the settlement wall. They couldn't have done that without the help of our own people."

"The mind control only works to control, not to retrieve." Hexxus' crazed laugh set my fangs on edge. "The Gretolics have been here since before the last war with the Nuttaki. How do you think that primitive race of insectiods obtained the nutrone to destroy the previous city of Huren?"

"Nutrone comes from the Jurigon Mountains," I seethed. "It was given to them by Clan Jurigon."

"Valose is not the only planet where nutrone exists."

My mind raced with the implications of the Gretolics secret existence. Had we wrongfully blamed Clan Jurigon for providing the Nuttaki with the power to destroy our city?

"You saw the Gretolics give the nutrone to the Nuttaki?"

"No, but—"

"So, you don't know for certain where it came from?" The interrogator roared within me. "Don't give me assumptions, Hexxus. I need facts."

"I believe the Gretolics instigated the war as a diversion so they could land their spacecraft undetected. They've had plenty of time to study us. Now they know too much." Hexxus leaned forward despite the blade at his throat. "So, you see, that's why I have to find Sia Jakkar's plasma gun."

I shook my head at his irrational reasoning. Hexxus always struck me as being a touch on the mental side. I attributed it to his genius, but now he seemed to be a brigg short of a full rakk. "For what purpose do you need a plasma gun?"

"To destroy the spacecraft before the Gretolics figure out

for themselves how to power up the nutrillium in their main engine thrusters." The longer Hexxus talked, the more his eyes glazed over and the less sense he made. "I've managed, thus far, to keep it non-operational, but that won't last. They're too smart. They'll eventually figure it out for themselves. Then it will be too late. They will take them, and then they will be gone forever."

"Who will be gone forever?" Chills raced over my scales in a flash of white.

Insanity shielded him from fearing for his life as Hexxus swatted away my deadly blade with a casual hand, but I allowed him to stand and wander around the room. He babbled on about boosting the energy levels of nutrillium while searching Sia Jakkar's desk, opening drawers, and looking under the furniture for a plasma weapon brought back from one of Sia Sakkar's travels to the stars.

"Where would he have hidden it?" Hexxus turned wild eyes on me and tilted his head. "Your shawra glows anew."

I smacked his hand away before he could touch me. I knew the whereabouts of the plasma gun, but I wasn't about to tell Hexxus. The male was completely out of his mind.

"Who will be gone forever, Hexxus?" I thought of the females Marie saw locked in cages.

"The males being held on the prison level."

I remained mute a moment over the shock of his words. "And the females?"

"What females?" Hexxus looked at me sideways.

He was either too crazy to remember, or he didn't know about the females at all. "The males being held," I diverted, "What are the Gretolics planning to do with them?"

"They are to be taken to a planet called, Tirius, in exchange for something called kript. And Sia Sakkar is among them."

I recoiled so hard at his words that I took a step back. "What is the kript for?"

"I don't know."

Annoyed that I had more questions than answers, I rushed Hexxus, slamming him against the wall. "Why are the Gretolics taking apart Sia Sakkar's spacecraft? Why don't they just use it to leave?"

"It's only a short-ranged skiff. They wouldn't get very far. And they need parts to fix their larger spacecraft."

"It's your creation." I slammed him against the wall again, rattling his teeth. "Make it long-ranged."

"No," Hexxus vehemently shook his head. "I didn't design the craft. It was given to Sia Sakkar by the Gretolics under the guise of goodwill. When in reality, Sia Sakkar was being used as a mule to bring back ingredients needed to make stasis."

"The blue liquid in the vials?"

"Yes. *Yes!*" Hexxus' eyes went wild. "They need it to keep the males healthy while they slumber."

"How would Sia Sakkar know of this *liquid?*"

"He didn't. Sia Sakkar wasn't exploring the stars as everyone thought. He was never alone on his travels. There were always Gretolics present." Hexxus locked eyes with me in a moment of clarity. "You must leave before they find you. You must get a message to Sia Jakkar. We can't let the Gretolics leave this planet with those males. Take this and place it on the dome."

"What is it?" I shied away from the circular device he thrust at me.

"A power diverter." Hexxus pushed the device at me. "It will displace the dome's shielding to create a door. A portable gate, if you will." Hexxus' eyes grew soft as his gaze floated past my shoulder. "So, you and your female can get out of the city."

Marie had crept so silently out of the hatch that I hadn't heard her approach. She reached out a hand and allowed Hexxus to place the device in her palm.

"It's our chance to escape, Draggar," Marie reasoned. "Come with us?" She nodded at Hexxus.

"I can't." He backed away, feverishly shaking his silvery mane. "I have to stay here and continue to thwart their attempts at powering up their craft."

"Okay," Marie spoke decisively. "Good luck to you, and thanks. Come on, Draggar, let's get the hell out of here."

Hexxus' eyes glazed over before darting around. Then he began to mumble incoherently to himself. Marie was right. It was time to go. Hexxus was proving to be an unreliable source of information. None of what he told me could be trusted.

"Tell Sia Jakkar everything I told you," Hexxus called after us as we exited out the tunnel and closed the hatch behind us.

Chapter Eighteen

MARIE

"I don't know how, but I can feel you didn't believe any of the shit that guy, Hexxus, told you."

"You're correct," Draggar said, crawling behind me in the dark tunnel with only a soft glowing rock to light our way. "It's the bond of our spirits that echoes within you. Like right now, I can sense your anxiety."

"Yeah. Crawling through a dark, dirt tunnel with no end in sight will do that to a girl," I tossed over my shoulder. "Where does this tunnel lead to anyway? I feel like we've been crawling for days."

"We've nearly reached the end." Draggar reached out and ran his finger across the arch of my foot, and I hurried ahead.

The handsome devil had discovered my ticklish spots while we romped around in Jakkar's bed. I glanced back to find a naughty half-grin tugging at his full upper lip.

A playful swirl spun around my heart. I always believed in Lily's reasoning for wanting to stay with Jakkar, even when the others looked at her like she lost her mind.

Now that I was experiencing it for myself, every negative thought I had about men and relationships vanished.

Draggar was my soulmate. It took my abduction and crashing on a new world to find him. But I had, and here we were, together, crawling our way to freedom.

"End of the road," I announced when the tunnel dead ended.

Draggar crowded me as he pushed at a wooden panel overhead. I couldn't resist wrapping my arms around his tight waist. He paused in his lifting to wrap his massive arms around me. I nuzzled the valley between his pecs and sighed.

"Can't we just stay down here forever?" I closed my eyes and absorbed his warmth. "I have a feeling nothing good is gonna happen once we resurface."

"I promise to get us out of Huren, nula." Snuggle time ended with a brief kiss, and Draggar went back to lifting the wooden panel above our heads.

I nodded and swallowed hard. Granted, he was built like a brick shithouse and was a total badass with those swords. There was only one of him and hundreds of the enemy awaiting us above ground.

Not that I didn't think he would do everything he could to keep me safe. I didn't want him to die trying.

It took a hard shove before dirt and light spilled on top of us. I sucked back the Downy freshness of the air. For whatever reason, Valose smelled as if it'd just come fresh from the dryer.

We waited a moment before Draggar poked the tip of his sword up through the hole, followed by his head. "All clear."

We emerged next to the dome's perimeter. The twin blue suns sat low in the sky, preparing to set. Time had felt so fleeting as we bonded beneath the sheets. It was hard to believe we spent an entire night and day inside Jakkar's private space.

"Here goes nothing," I mumbled, placing the device Hexxus gave us on the translucent shielding of the dome.

Nothing happened. Not even a ripple. I tentatively touched the dome before flattening my palm against the warm shield. It remained solid, impenetrable.

"Well, shit," I cursed and removed the device to hand to Draggar. "Here. You try. Maybe I'm not doing it right."

"Hexxus just said to place it on the dome, and the power would be displaced for us to exit."

I looked around the city as Draggar examined the device, turning it over in his hands. The palace's beauty was hard to look away from, but I needed to watch our backs.

The lifeless landscape was a ruse. Plenty was going on inside the hangar and on the lower levels under the palace.

A flash of silver hair drew my attention to the entrance of the small cottage where we hid. It was Hexxus emerging. He didn't look back to where we were but kept going toward the hanger.

A group of Gretolics exited the hanger, proceeded by two zombified Valosian males. The exchange between Hexxus was nothing special until one of the Gretolics looked hard in our direction.

"Hexxus lied." Draggar pounded the dome with a meaty fist. "It isn't a portable gate, as he claimed. The device doesn't work."

"We need to go." I tugged on Draggar's arm.

"He set us up!"

"I don't think so." I backed up only to hit my back on the dome. "Looks like he's trying to slow them down."

Hexxus had tackled the Gretolic who spotted us to the ground. He was now being hauled up and his wrists bound by the two Valosian males acting as bodyguards.

One Gretolic spoke words into its wrist device, and more Valosian males emerged from the hanger. A spindly arm pointed in our direction, and we were being descended upon by a whole group of males.

Draggar switched into defensive mode, lifting me from the ground as they barreled down on us. The option of crawling back down our hole was scratched when a pair broke off to enter the cottage. They would be headed right for us.

"Wrap your arms and legs around me and hold on tight," Draggar commanded and took off at a sprint.

Swords unsheathed, he led with the points, daring anyone to get too close as we were quickly surrounded. The Valosians came to the fight empty-handed. My guess was the Gretolics didn't trust their puppets enough to weaponize them.

Draggar slashed and swung at everything that moved. The circle of males closed around us, Draggar spinning one way and then the other to keep from being taken from behind.

"Use my harness as a strap and lash yourself to my body."

The exploding aggression of his soul within me became focused with determination, and I wondered what he suddenly decided.

"Why?" I asked the question, but did as he commanded, binding myself to his body with his sword harness.

"I'll need my arms to swim."

"Oh, shit!" We were escaping through the recirculating pipe in the fountain. That wasn't good news for me. "Oh, shit..."

Draggar rushed the circle between two of the smallest males. Swords up, I could feel his compassion for the males. He wouldn't hurt them unless he were given no other choice.

"I need you to trust me, Marie," Draggar said while running full tilt toward the fountain in the city's center. "I feel your anxiety, but I need you to let that go and open yourself up to me. Our spirits need to coalesce so I can hang onto your essence if you don't make it through the length of the pipe."

"If I don't make it?" I repeated. "You mean if I drown?"

My body began to shake uncontrollably as I faced off with

knowing the mechanism of my death. Death by drowning. I guess there were more gruesome ways to go, but drowning wouldn't have been my first choice.

"I need you to calm." How could Draggar's voice sound so serene as he sprinted across the ground with a group of males chasing after us? "Our spirits must join."

"I thought spirits only joined during sex. How're we planning on doing that?"

"Initially. Once our shawras appear, we can join our spirits anytime, but you must close your eyes. Let go, and reach out to me. I'll be there waiting to embrace you."

I closed my eyes and tried to think happy thoughts. Yet, this was the craziest shit I had ever heard of.

I experienced the tangible connection every time we had sex. I could even feel his hyped-up energy spinning around inside me now. But, to close my eyes and be with him in spirit?

It still seemed like a magically fictitious thing to do. The moment I let myself go and gave myself over to trust, warmth speared me in the center of my chest and spread outward, running the length of my limbs.

Draggar's presence was strong and soothing. His spirit was there, reaching for me as he'd promised. I latched onto him, twinning my soul with his.

"Take a deep breath and hold it when I say," he whispered close to my ear.

Or had I only heard his voice inside my head?

Either way, I answered out loud. "Okay. Just say when."

I held tight around his neck; my ankles crossed at the small of his back to hold me in place. Draggar's body bounced with his long, heavy strides, eating up the distance between the males chasing us and my inevitable demise.

I concentrated on keeping my breathing steady and even.

Focusing inward on Draggar's confident spinning of energy dancing with mine.

The echo of his painful past haunted the edges of his essence, but it didn't feel as if he dwelled on the loss of his first spirit mate and his daughter. He'd accepted it, mourned it, and had moved on. With me.

My heart fluttered with joy. At the same time, stuttered with fear as we drew closer to the fountain.

It was so strange to feel this close to someone. As if we shared the same mind, the same skin.

"Deep breath, nula, and hold it for as long as you can," Draggar ordered before tossing his swords down with a clang.

With a solid leap, we became airborne. With a hard splash, Draggar dove us into the fountain. When I first saw the sparkling water, I wanted to take a dip. Now? Not so much.

The water was a lot deeper than I'd anticipated. My ears popped with Draggar's firm strokes, taking us deeper and deeper until we were swept up in a current.

The breath I was holding grew tight in my lungs. I blew out a few bubbles to ease the pressure. The desire to let it all loose and inhale was overwhelming.

I squeezed Draggar tighter. In turn, his spirit hugged mine. I fought back my rising panic and the need to struggle out of his hold to save myself. Draggar's internal calmness soothed me even as his arms and legs churned through the water like an Olympic swimmer.

I could hold on. I wouldn't freak out. I released more bubbles.

The longer we remained underwater, the more my lungs burned. The more my throat convulsed, wanting to blow out what little air filled my lungs and take a nice, deep breath to replenish my lack of oxygen.

There was nothing to breathe. If I filled my lungs with water, I would die.

Draggar's spirit wove around mine until I couldn't tell where his began and where mine ended. We were one.

He knew I was close to the end. He'd said as long as he could hold onto my spirit, he could save me once we reached the end of the pipe.

I held on for a few more seconds, then the inevitable happened, and the reflex to breathe took control. I expelled what little oxygen was left and sucked in gulps of water.

My body jerked as my eyes flew open. My lungs grew heavy. My vision dimmed. Streams of Draggar's silvery hair ribboned out behind as his powerful arms pulled us through the tunnel.

The warmth of his soul kept me warm as the darkness closed in around me.

Chapter Nineteen

DRAGGAR

I knew the moment my spirit mate suffocated. Her spirit relaxed and waved lazily in my hold. She wasn't gone yet. I clung to her essence, not allowing her to pass into the Realm of the Spirits.

It was cheating death, but I refused to lose another spirit mate.

As long as I could keep her spirit with me, I could revive her later. But there was a limit to how long her body could be deprived of oxygen.

I quickened my strokes and forged ahead. Dim at first, the light at the end of the pipe grew brighter with every firm kick and pull of my arms.

Marie's body hung loosely from where she was attached to me by my sword harness. Her limbs flopped against me as I swam us out of the pipe and into the Twien River.

We surfaced, and I rolled to my back, making sure Marie's head was above the lood. I thanked the Spirits and with a quick look around, floated us toward a rocky section of the bank where the floratrap could not grow.

This couldn't have been a more perfect spot. The

floratrap field could be used as a shield against predators, but I still needed a safe place to pass the dark hurs to care for Marie.

I backstroked to the rocky side of the river that ran along a cluster of small caves while keeping an eye on the carnivorous foliage, which remained deceptively still. Then pulled Marie's limp body across a flat rock.

The life of her spirit was waning, yet she fought to stay with me. I had to get air into her lungs and make her heart beat again.

Keeping a keen eye on my surroundings, I raised above her, drew in a deep breath, placed my mouth over hers, and forced my air into her lungs.

Falling back on the survival skills taught to all warriors, I placed the palm of my hand over where I'd felt her heart once beat and began to pump. I switched off between pumping her chest and giving her breaths.

Another forced breath, then two, and her hands flailed at her sides. I felt the stirring of her spirit within me and smiled. I turned her onto her side, where she spewed the lood filling her lungs.

Her eyes were wide and wildly dazed as she sucked back air. I gathered her in my arms and ran for the mouth of a cave. Located just inside Nuttaki territory, this region had long been abandoned since the horde had moved farther southwest to avoid the encroaching floratrap.

Just before I ducked inside, Marie pointed up and spoke a name in a raspy voice, "Amy."

I followed her finger's direction and crouched low to hide us from the Gretolic conveyance flying overhead. It was like the ones lined up on the training field.

It bobbled as if the operator were new to flying and headed northwest, out toward the islands off the coast of the Jurigon Mountains.

A flag of the same bright mane as Amy's hung down one side of the vessel while the one doing the flying blew around his head in a silvery cloud.

I stepped farther into the cave, contemplating who had made it out of the city. I'd hoped it was Hexxus and wondered why he was taking the female to the uninhabited island.

At first, I thought Hexxus had betrayed us, but he hadn't. He saved us by trying to distract the Gretolics. As we were being chased, I saw him taken down by two males, cuffed, and dragged away.

I prayed to the Spirits that he got away and stole one of their vessels. He was a crazy fuck, but I didn't want to think about what they'd do to him for his betrayal.

Even though the device he gave us hadn't worked, I still had it tucked away in the pocket of my kiltus in hopes Zikkar could figure out how it worked.

I had much to tell Sia Jakkar. However, I didn't know how much of what Hexxus said was actual or fictitious nonsense. All I knew for certain was an attack on the Gretolic needed to be planned and quickly.

Hexxus had warned that the Gretolics would figure out how to power their ship and when they did, a hundredth males, including Sia Jakkar's twin brother, Sakkar, would be taken off-planet and exchanged for something called kript. I couldn't let that happen.

Inside the cave, I found a niche that would do nicely to hide us from any predators that might be following the river. Marie snuggled into me and shivered. Exhausted from her ordeal, she was asleep in secs.

I was thrilled my spirit mate lived, but not with the situation we were in. The cave was damp and cooling fast from the lack of the suns' warmth.

I didn't regret tossing my swords aside to save my female,

but I wished I hadn't been put in the situation to have had to make that choice. I would always choose Marie over anything or anyone.

We were both soaked through, but I couldn't start a fire without giving away our position. So, I huddled inside the niche with my precious cargo, piled her in my lap, and rubbed at her cold limbs.

My ears twitched and swiveled for even the slightest of sounds as I put my sensitive auditory system to work. As the nocturnal jungle came alive in the dark, my mind went to work on the best route out of Nuttaki territory and the safest way through the floratrap field.

Chapter Twenty

MARIE

At first, I thought I was dreaming. The ceiling in my apartment wasn't made of stone, and neither were the walls. On Earth, I wouldn't be waking up to a powerful male body holding me so protectively while my fingers were entwined in strands of his silvery hair.

Draggar shifted beneath me, and a swirl of warmth hugged me on the inside. "You're awake. How do you feel?"

"Warm and snuggly, but tired." I sifted my fingers through his bunny-soft hair and nuzzled his muscled pec I was using for a pillow. "I think I might have drooled on you a little."

"You are welcome to drool on me anytime." Draggar's chest rumbled in amusement.

Then I remembered something!

My belly swam when I lifted my head too fast. The deviled egg flying above us had a passenger with fiery red hair. "Amy. Who would have taken her? Do you think she's okay?"

"I don't know the answer to either question, but I hope it was Hexxus." Draggar shifted again. "And the craft headed to an uninhabited island chain."

"Then we should go there and find her." I scrambled to rise, but the ceiling was too low.

Draggar gently pulled me back into his embrace as easily as he would have a naughty kitten. "Calm yourself, nula. You still need to rest." The echo of his spirit gently swirled around mine in a soothing dance. "I have no means to reach the islands. Even if we had a raft to float us there, the squidlin would swallow us whole before we ever made it off the shore."

"Surely, someone has been over there before."

"To my knowledge, the islands remain unexplored."

"You have landmasses on this planet that are uncharted?"

"Yes, several." Draggar stood, hunched over in the niche, and carried me out to the cave's main chamber. Standing tall, he cracked his back while stretching his legs. "From what we can see with a scope from the eastern shore, there are similar islands that lay hundredths of milose away in the Caspeen Sea."

"That blows my friggin' mind." I shook my head while he walked us around the interior of the small cave. That niche was tight and as tall he was, I imagined he'd been cramped. "As advanced as some of the technology you guys have here, I can't believe you have no way to cross your seas. There's nothing on Earth left untouched by humans. Well, except maybe deep down in the ocean."

"Why haven't you explored this *deep down in the ocean*?" he grumbled.

"I meant no offense." His spirit had tensed and curled as if slighted. "And we haven't explored the deepest parts of our oceans because we have no means to get there," I repeated his reason, feeling foolish.

Draggar harrumphed, grumbling like an old grizzly.

"I really didn't mean to offend you." I twirled my fingers

through strands of his incredible hair, hooding my eyes at him. "Maybe I can make it up to you somehow."

My sexy tone piqued his interest, but the rumble of my empty belly won his attention.

"The suns are on the rise." Draggar found a flat rock and set me down on it. "Stay inside the cave. I'll see if there's anything edible close by."

My fingers dug into the rock at the sight of his retreating back. I wanted to run after him, but I stayed where I was, reminding myself that Draggar wasn't anything like the people that had let me down on Earth.

I'd gone out on a limb and trusted him with—not only my life—but my very soul, and he hadn't disappointed me. Draggar had been there when I needed him the most. He'd more than earned my trust.

I cringed thinking of the burning suffocation I felt as the water filled my lungs. Even after my heart stopped beating, I remained aware of his presence. It'd been a vital essence that kept me grounded when all I wanted to do was fly apart in terror over my demise.

I rubbed at the scattering of goosebumps peppering my arms and looked around the cave for the first time. It was nothing more than a hollowed-out hole in the base of a low-slung mountain range.

At the mouth of the cave, the first rays of dawn spilled inside. I started to worry over all the quiet. I couldn't hear Draggar moving around outside at all.

I closed my eyes and reached inside myself to explore the other half of me, floating languidly around my heart. It was like having an internal GPS on Draggar's emotions. At the moment, he was calm.

At the first sound of footsteps, I opened my eyes as Draggar entered the cave, holding a large leaf shaped like a bowl in one hand and a bunch of large berries that looked like giant grapes in the other.

"Floratrap berries." Draggar held up one and then the other. "Lood from the river outside."

"I thought those things were killer plants."

"They are, but the fruit they produce grows at the end of their roots." Draggar brought his findings over to me. "The roots can't harm you unless you come into contact with them. They have thin fibers that can attach to flesh and suck your blood."

"I think I ran into those things before I dropped into the mine shaft." I sniffed at the berries he offered me. "I tried to hang on to these slimy roots that had thorns poking into the palms of my hands."

"That was them." Draggar bit into a huge berry and chewed around his words. "Their roots can run just beneath the surface for milose. That's how their fields spread so quickly. I felt the sting of their fibers when I jumped in the hole after you."

I bit into a berry and moaned. The skin was a little tough and bitter, but the inside was like a juicy mango. "Why don't you guys get rid of them if they're so dangerous?" I swiped away a stream of sweet juice running down my chin.

"Why would we exterminate the indigenous species on our planet?" Draggar raised an eyebrow in question. "Floratrap is definitely dangerous. One stole my first spirit mate away from me, but every living thing on Valose serves a greater purpose that keeps the planet in balance. Like the floratrap. They produce oxygen and purify the air."

I swallowed the last bite of one berry and picked up another. "Earth could take a few lessons from you guys. We've fucked up our planet beyond repair."

Draggar grunted. "Then I'm glad you were stolen away and brought here. To me."

"Me too." I grinned as he passed me the leaf bowl filled with water and drank. "I've changed so much since crash-landing here."

"You're more resilient than even I gave you credit for," Draggar admitted, taking back the water bowl. "I was concerned for your mental fortitude when you were thrown into the fighting. With no training of any kind, you exhibited an inner strength of even the most seasoned warriors."

Tears sprang to my eyes. "You sure know how to make a girl's heart sigh." Setting aside my berries, I laid my hands over my heart. "I was broken when I came here. Inside." I patted my chest. "I'd built up a wall around myself. But you stripped me of my distrust and showed me that I could love without getting hurt."

Draggar ducked his head and peered up at me through soft eyes.

"So, thank you, Draggar, my silver seducer, for this new life. You saved me in more ways than one. You healed my soul."

Draggar moved to kneel at my feet, taking my hands in his much larger ones. "My spirit had grown dark from the loss of my first spirit mate. I never thought I'd ever feel anything but loss for the rest of my suns-rises. Until I found you, so it was you, my tiny warrior, who saved me."

It was true. He crumbled my defenses, but there was one thing left between us, and I needed to come clean.

"I have something I want you to know," I began with a shaky voice. "You may not view me in the same light after I tell you."

"There's nothing you can say that would change how I feel about you, nula."

"I'm not as honorable as you think I am. I lied to Lily when we first met. I told her I was an accountant when I wasn't." Draggar's eyes narrowed, and I almost lost my nerve.

"I'm not brave, and I'm not a warrior. I'm a cocktail waitress in a skeevy nudie bar."

Draggar blinked up at me. "I don't understand all of your words. What is a-cow-tent?"

"Someone that works with numbers."

"And the other?"

I rubbed my forehead. How to explain a titty bar to an alien? "Well, back on Earth, I served drinks in a not-so-reputable establishment where women dance around naked for men in exchange for currency."

Draggar shook his head. "You don't give yourself enough credit. Your occupation doesn't define who you are as a person, Marie. What matters is what's on the inside. I've seen your spirit, and it's beautifully wild."

"So, you don't think less of me?"

He rose onto his knees and cupped my face in his hands. "I love you with my whole spirit. I could never think less of you."

"And I love you with everything I am."

I was so relieved that I sagged. I aired my dirty laundry, and Draggar still looked at me as if I was the most important thing on Valose.

Our meal forgotten, he lifted me off my rock-seat and sat down, parting my thighs, so I straddled his lap.

My emotions were raw and riding high. I needed an outlet for the burst of energy. Draggar's hardening cock was just the ticket.

I ripped my dress off over my head, tossing it to the floor. I fumbled with the clasp on Draggar's kilt, but he pushed my hands aside to unclip it and shoved the material separating us away.

Skin-to-scales, his body was hot and hard. I moaned, rubbing my hands up and down his powerful chest—his abs crunched in rippling cords.

My pulse thickened as our mouths met. Gentle at first, he nipped at my lips before plunging inside. His hands went everywhere at once, squeezing and kneading my flesh into a frenzy.

His fingers found my slit, dipping inside to test my wetness. "Your cunt weeps for me."

His dirty words hit me with a fresh wave of heat. "It does, but it's my turn to do the claiming," I said, slowly riding his thick appendages.

"Then lay claim to me, tiny warrior." Draggar leaned back against the wall, giving his body over to me. Pulling his fingers free of my pussy, he shot me a roguish grin and licked his fingers clean.

"You're a naughty male," I purred and wrapped my hand around his thick, alien cock. "Just the way I like you."

With my feet on the ground, I lined up his silver sex with mine. Lifting myself on tiptoes, I impaled myself on his massive erection in one swift stroke.

I cried out, and Draggar roared as his cock burned its way into my pussy. My head fell back, and my body arched. It felt so damn good to be this full, stretched to capacity.

I rocked my hips, grinding into his lap, and was rewarded with the triangular flaps at the base of his cock teasing my clit. I looked down at his erotic equipment and was stripped of all inhibitions.

I rode my warrior's cock with depravity born from pure lust. Our flesh slapped together as he thrust into me from beneath, and I crashed down from above.

This was nothing like the tender mating of our first time. This was about leaving a mark, claiming what was mine.

Everything about him excited me. The crunching of his abs when he rolled his hips. The bunching of his hard muscles beneath my greedy hands. The fierce gleam in his eyes while we fucked. The wicked swirl of his spirit as it danced with mine.

My thoughts scattered as white-hot flames licked behind my eyes. My pussy clenched in waves around his swelling cock. My inner muscles working to milk him for every drop of his hot seed splashing inside me.

He kissed me gently in the aftermath of our turbulent coupling. My pussy throbbed from being used so roughly, but I had no regrets. After experiencing the icy fingers of death, I needed wild and abandoned. I needed to feel alive.

Chapter Twenty-One

DRAGGAR

I t was bittersweet leaving our cave behind. It had been a haven much like my skypod where we could rest and mate without worry that a predator, or an enemy, could easily intrude.

I was well-rested and wholly relaxed from all the sex and sharing of our spirits. The echo of Marie was stronger than ever within me. It had been so long since I felt another's essence that I hadn't realized how alone I truly felt.

That ache of solitude was now filled to overflowing with the blustery passion that was my Marie. She had so much life in her. I was swept up in the maelstrom that was her.

"It will be safer for us to swim out of the floratrap field," I said to Marie, who was clinging to my shoulders as I quietly swam us up the Twien River. "Once the field thins, we'll skirt the edge of the jungle and head to the coast. There's a back entrance into the Caverns of the Ancients."

"Sounds easy enough."

"As long as we stay close to the rocks and as far away from the blooms as possible," I added. There was nothing easy about a stroll across Valose. "The tentacles can reach out for many fates, so stay alert for any thick vines moving our way."

Marie tensed, and I could feel her looking around as she kept hold of my shoulders. "Got it."

"Keep watch for any Nuttaki, too. I don't believe they would venture this far north, but you never know with them."

"Roger that," Marie said. "Nuttaki and deadly vines. Anything else?"

There was plenty. I didn't feel it was in Marie's best interest to rattle off the entire list of predatory species we could possibly encounter.

About an hur into our swim, the floratrap field gave way to the jungle's large leaves. I swam us around in a wide circle, scanning the area before walking us up onto the shore.

"I think my fingers are permanently pruned." Marie examined the strange wrinkles on her fingertips.

"Why didn't I grab the medic pack before we left the city?" I cursed myself.

"This is normal when I stay in the water too long," Marie explained as I examined her deformed flesh.

"Normal?"

"It will go away after I dry off." Marie shivered.

I rubbed her arms and shoulders to warm her. "Once we reach the back entrance of the caverns, I think it would be safe enough to build a fire to warm you."

"I'm fine." Marie's eyes darted around, searching for the source of every tiny noise coming from the jungle. "Let's just get the hell out of here and find someplace safe."

Her anxiety swirled inside my gut. My spirit mate presented a brave front, but she was trembling on the inside. She was correct. We couldn't remain in one place for very long.

I kept her hand in mine as we skirted the jungle along the coast. Up ahead, the Jurigon Mountains pierced the silvery sky with its jagged peaks. Clouds clung to the azure caps in wispy tendrils.

Rustling swiveled my ears in a direction up ahead. I signaled for Marie to crouch low, using the leafy underbrush as cover. We listened and waited.

Nuttaki!

Stealth was not a skill they possessed. By the sound of their spindly legs scurrying over the debris-littered jungle, I'd guess there were twenty.

Instinctively, I reached over my shoulders for my swords and came up empty handed. I'd left them in the city to save my spirit mate.

So, we had two choices. We could hide and hope they didn't sniff us out with their pointed beaks, or I could wait for the perfect moment and attack them before they knew what hit them.

I could have easily cut them down with my swords. Hand to hand wasn't impossible, but Nuttaki were tough to kill. Their bodies were covered in an exoskeleton that acted as natural armor. On each of their eight spindly legs were points as sharp as any warrior's dagger.

I would gladly lay down my own life to protect Marie. But then what would become of her? A lone female in the jungle on Valose was as good as dead. Even if she survived to make it to the back entrance of the caverns by some miracle, she wouldn't know how to open the secret passage to get inside.

I gestured for Marie to follow. We kept low and moved farther into the jungle and away from the approaching Nuttaki. My spirit mate was wise to step where I stepped, so we silently crept across the debris-littered ground.

I moved a large leaf aside and froze.

The patooga looked as surprised to see me as I was him. Feasting on a meal of decaying rexose, it raised and prepared to pounce. I shoved a gasping Marie behind me and fell into a battle stance. Weaponless. What else could I do but give this beast the fight of its life?

The glint of Valosian steel sparkled off to my left. I couldn't believe my eyes. There. Still stuck in the rexose's tough hide was Trisso's sword.

I sent up a silent thanks to Trisso and the Spirits watching our backs.

"Stay down and out of sight." I pushed a trembling Marie behind the trunk of a giant thriose tree and formed a plan of how to get my hands on Trisso's sword.

Chapter Twenty-Two

MARIE

I could have shit myself when that saber-toothed tiger made that unexpected appearance. Draggar's spirit sparked electric but otherwise remained cool, calm, and collected.

As I hid behind the trunk of a giant, prehistoric-looking tree, Draggar made his move. Every movement, every step looked practiced as he faced off with the enormous cat-beast.

I'd seen the guys fight one of these things before. It took four of them, armed with swords, to take it down. However, Draggar was weaponless, and there was only one of him. Within me, I felt no echo of fear from him, just a calculating determination.

I didn't see it at first. As Draggar inched closer to the dead rexose, I recognized what was sticking out of its bluish hide. The hilt of a Valosian warrior's sword.

Draggar circled in a dangerous dance with the patooga, step by cautious step, bringing him closer to the hilt. He was going for the sword, and I silently cheered him on.

The world stood still as I held my breath. Draggar's eyes darted to me and widened. A flare of panic surged through the echo of his spirit. The little hairs on the back of my neck stood at attention, and my muscles seized.

Something was behind me, but I was too afraid to look. I'd faced my death once already with my eyes wide open. I didn't want to see what was coming for me next. I'd rather my last sight be of Draggar's too handsome, scarred face.

Before I knew what was happening, Draggar rushed the patooga. The beast crouched low and pounced. Its enormous paws tipped with unsheathed claws were out and at the ready to shred Draggar to ribbons.

Draggar threw his arms out and dove for the sword's hilt. The patooga missed him by a breath as Draggar hit the ground and rolled away.

When Draggar rebounded to his feet, he wielded the sword. He came barreling toward me.

The patooga skidded around, its hindlegs slipping on the ground, kicking up a cloud of blue dust. Then it was tight on Draggar's heels. And it was coming right for us.

My fingers clawed into the tree trunk. My heart thudded in my ears. My body bloomed with sweat waiting and watching for Draggar's next step.

He caught me around the waist as he dove through the air, taking my body down with his. The breath in my lungs blasted as my back slammed to the ground.

Draggar rolled over at the last second and speared the lunging patooga in the belly. Using the sword and the beast's momentum, he flung the patooga over our heads and into the encroaching horde of Nuttaki I'd felt creeping up behind me.

Draggar didn't hang around to see what came next. He tossed me over his shoulder, plowing his way through the jungle using his found sword as a machete to cut a trail through the thick foliage.

From my place over Draggar's broad shoulder, I had a

clear view of the patooga chomping down on the Nuttaki as it bellied up to a buffet.

The patooga yelped. A Nuttaki's spindly leg still hung from its lip as it was plucked from the ground by its hindleg. Dangling above the jungle by a thick vine, a mammoth bloom of an iridescent blue peeled back its glorious petals and dropped the patooga into its gaping yawn. The petals closed around the patooga in a deadly cocoon.

"Ohmygod! That shit just happened," I murmured.

"What?" Draggar asked but didn't look back, forging ahead.

"The patooga ate the Nuttaki, and then a floratrap ate the patooga."

"It happens."

"Okaaaay. So that's a common occurrence." I raised my eyebrows. "This planet is going to take some getting used to. I think you can slow down now. We're not being chased."

"Not taking any more chances with you." Draggar didn't slow. "I'll slow when we reach the back entrance to the Caverns of the Ancients."

I bounced around on Draggar's shoulder for what felt like miles until we reached the base of the spectacular mountain range I'd only seen from a distance. With a pronounced limp, he walked us around to the mouth of a cave.

"You're hurt." I wriggled in his hold. "I think you can put me down now."

"I swore to protect you, and that's what I plan to do. I'll put you down once we're safely inside the cavern."

There was no point in arguing with my fierce, bullheaded warrior. I did try to get a look at what was going on with his leg. Blue blood covered his right thigh, and I gasped. He'd been running with that nasty gash the entire way.

"Draggar." I tapped him on the shoulder. "Don't you think we should stop and dress that wound?"

"I'll be fine. It's just a scratch."

We entered the mouth of a cave with Draggar still carrying me like a sack of flour.

"How is this a back entrance?" I peered around. "We've reached a dead-end."

"Only at first glance," Draggar grunted. "You have to know where to look."

Draggar walked to the back of the cave and finally set me on my feet. He tucked his fingers inside what first appeared to be a crevice in the rock wall and pushed.

Muscles bulging and straining, the wall turned out to be a door. The slab gave way and slid to one side, revealing a black abyss beyond.

"Yeah. Another dark and scary place." I quipped and rolled my eyes.

"Dark but not scary." Draggar blinked a translucent lens over both eyes, enabling him to see in the dark. "Hold onto my hand, and I'll lead you through."

I stood and waited while Draggar muscled the stone panel closed, then we were on our way down the black tunnel.

It was so dark, the only thing I could see was the glowing patterns marking Draggar's chest and arms. I hated not being able to see what was in front of me, but I trusted Draggar. I knew he would never purposely lead me into danger.

We walked forever. With every step, Draggar's limp grew worse until his gait was grossly lopsided.

"Draggar." I tried to drag my feet to get him to stop. "I know you're a badass and all, but we need to stop and do something with your leg."

"We're almost there, nula," he gritted out. "Almost there."

I could just imagine his face set in a fierce mask in the velvety darkness. The echo of his spirit was no longer fluid but thickened in pain.

A few more steps, and I was ready to protest when a flash

of light blinded me, leaving behind bright dots with every hard blink.

It was a torch being held by an imposing figure standing in shadow. Draggar sagged against the rock wall.

"Well, it's about time you got here," the male joked. "What took you so long, old warrior?"

It was Nekko! Jakkar's second in command.

"Ran into a little trouble," Draggar huffed and shoved at Nekko's shoulder.

"I hate to break up the bromance, but Draggar needs to have his leg checked out. Where's Nullar?"

Nekko gave me a quick once over before returning his attention to Draggar and locking onto his shawra. "Fierce little spirit mate you've got there."

"What she lacks in stature, she makes up for in the sharp whip of her tongue."

Nekko threw his head back in uproarious laughter. "I'm glad you're finally getting back what you've been dishing out."

I was done playing around while my warrior bled to death. "His leg," I demanded, "Medical attention. Now would be good."

"As you command." Nekko bowed with a flourish.

"And I can do without the theatrics."

Nekko smirked and gave Draggar a sideways look before turning to lead the way. The tunnel went on a few more feet before opening into a massive cavern. A huge fire pit took center stage, flickering warm light on the murals decorating the walls.

I stopped in my tracks with my mouth hanging open. The rock ceiling inside rose to a daunting height. It was the biggest cave I'd ever seen in my damn life, with small caves carved out at regular intervals along the opposite wall.

Our arrival must have been anticipated because all the girls I'd been abducted with began to step out of the little caves. Jakkar followed Lily. She took one look at me, threw out her arms, and ran toward me. I did the same, and we collided in the middle.

"I'm so sorry for being such a giant bitch to you," I blubbered. "It's just my fucked-up way of dealing with shit."

"I know, and it's okay." Lily hugged me tighter. "I'm so happy to see you."

"Me too. There were times that I didn't think we'd make it here. But Draggar is a superhero and saved my life too many times for me to count." I pulled away and looked around the cave for him. "He's hurt and needs Nullar to patch up his leg."

Lily pointed over my shoulder, and I turned around to find Draggar already being treated. His eyes locked with mine, and he nodded that he was okay. The echo of his spirit had relaxed and contently swirled around mine. I sagged into Lily's hold. We were finally safe.

She led me over to the fire in the center of the cave and sat down.

"What of Amy?" Lily's lips thinned, and her eyes darkened with concern.

Guilt washed over me. "I'm so sorry, Lily. I shouldn't have left her, but I had a chance to get away from Rayyar, and I took it. I swear I was headed back to the settlement to get help for her when I fell into a hole."

"You don't need to apologize, Marie." Lily brushed my hair back from my face. "I know you did what you could."

"Still, I should have done more." The other girls began to gather around me. "After Draggar got us out of the city, I saw her being flown in a Gretolic vessel by a Valosian male. I didn't get a look at who he was. We think it was Hexxus escaping."

"You were inside the city of Huren?" Isobel looked dumbfounded. "What was it like?"

"I thought it was domed off. How'd you get inside?" Willow asked.

Elise nodded and pointed at Willow, wanting to know the answer. The poor girl was mute. I'd given her a hard time when we first met.

I was no longer the same bitch I once was. Everything I died and lived through had changed me. I was still me, only a better version.

I looked her in the eyes and laid my hands on her shoulders. "I owe you an apology."

She adamantly shook her head and signed something with her hands.

"No. I'm serious." I waved away her protest. "I was mean to you when we first met, and I'm so freaking sorry. Can you forgive me so we can be friends?"

Elise nodded. Her bottom lip trembled before she threw her arms around my neck and squeezed.

"That goes for all of you," I said, still hugging Elise. "I can't totally curb my smart-assed mouth, but we've all been through hell together."

"And what better way to bond than through an alien abduction," Isobel smirked.

"I know, right. I think of you all as my friends. Even Layla. Although she's a traitorous bitch." I let go of Elise and sat back. "Draggar taught me that some people are too ignorant for their own good and need saving from themselves."

"True," Lily added. "I hate that she got you and Amy involved in whatever stupid shit she thought would benefit her by releasing Rayyar."

"I hope... they're okay," Rose said through halted breaths. "Marie. Please don't...hate me. You like...Aggar. Only platonic. He thinks...of me...as a sister."

I touched the bandage wrapped around her ribcage. "I know. Lily told me. You're okay now?"

"Broken ribs...collapsed lung...almost healed," she smiled. "Thanks...to Nullar."

"I'm not jealous anymore about Aggar. He was a passing fancy." I stood in the center of my new friends and tugged the front of my ruined dress down. "Tell me the truth, ladies. Does this shawra make my ass look fat?"

A collective gasp echoed around the tunnel. Lily clapped, her eyes glazing over with tears. Isobel and Willow went slack jawed. Elise moved in for a closer look. And Rose smiled the happiest grin.

"Sit your ass down and tell us everything." Isobel tugged me down with a lopsided grin. "Don't spare any of the juicy details."

I was starving and in dire need of a bath, but I laughed and started from the beginning. The girls hung on my every word as I recapped our epic adventure. Then began to chatter around me in awe of what we'd been through to get here.

I looked over at Draggar, now deep in conversation with Jakkar and Nekko. I knew they were formulating a plan of attack to free their males and rescue the caged women.

Draggar gestured toward Lily, and Jakkar's eyes landed on his mate. I knew he was explaining about Amy and how we saw her being flown over to an island.

Then Draggar handed the device Hexxus gave us to Zikkar, who flipped it over and over in his hands, studying it intently. He fluffed his hands through his silver hair as if describing Hexxus' frazzled appearance.

Zikkar's face paled as Draggar spoke quickly, telling all that Hexxus had said. The kernels of truth would have to be teased out of all the crazy shit the male had told, yet nothing could be discounted.

I was afraid for my warrior. Afraid for all the males that would be bravely taking up arms against their new enemy. They were in for the fight of their lives.

We had a long journey ahead of us, fraught with unknown dangers. The warriors would forge ahead, and in the end, I knew they would emerge victorious.

As I sat in the circle of my new friends, I knew this was only a temporary reprieve from what lay ahead. I wouldn't be leaving. My warrior was here, and I was in it for the long haul.

Draggar's silvery gaze caught and held mine. Valose might be the scariest place I had ever been, but a life without my silver seducer would be an even scarier place.

Not the End!
Silver Savior
Warriors of Valose Saga 3
Is Next!

Next Up!

SILVER SAVIOR: WARRIORS OF VALOSE SAGA 3

Silver Savior
Warriors of Valose Saga 3

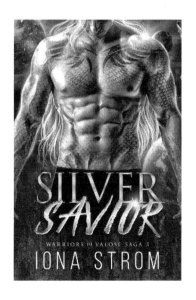

Amy

I had been abducted by aliens, survived a crash-landing in a spaceship--none of which I, thankfully, remembered. Then, an alien medic--who looked like an elf from *The Lord of the Rings*--miraculously healed my injuries in record time. I made it through all that and even a trek through a deadly jungle to relative safety.

Just when I was beginning to feel like myself, I was whacked over the head and--once again--abducted. Only this time I knew my abductor, but catastrophe struck, and I was left on my own in the wilds of the jungle with only my wits to keep me alive. Injured and weaponless, how long would I last on my own?

Maxxon

After my colleague and I stumbled upon the unimaginable, he was brutally murdered before my very eyes. I managed to escape the city of Huren before I succumbed to the same fate, taking with me the truth of the gray invaders.

In the jungle, I found the impossible. As a Royal Medic, I had treated everything from common ailments to gravely injured warriors with extreme proficiency, but the unconscious female in my arms had me baffled. She was definitely another species. What was more shocking was the call of her spirit to mine.

AMAZON

Silver Savior: Warriors of Valose Saga 3

PROLOGUE (TEN MUNTHIS PAST) MAXXON

Blood had spurted from Kayyot's throat in a blue fountain. Cold, unseeing eyes had stared out of the male's face doing the slicing. Gretolics, the gray aliens, were in control of the male's actions and in control of the city of Huren.

My scales had blanched white. My throat had worked hard to swallow the gurgle of bile that threatened to spew. It wasn't because of the gore I'd left behind. As a Royal Medic, I'd seen plenty and far worse battle wounds, warriors with severed limbs that needed to be reattached, deep gashes displaying the bone beneath in need of sutures.

No, it wasn't the yawning slice across the male's throat that made me want to heave. It was the loss of my friend and colleague that made me ill.

So much deceit. So much death. So many lies.

I held tight to the truth in my hands as I sprinted down the hallway and careened around the next corner, hoping to lose my pursuers. When they'd surprised us in the secret lab Kayyot, and I had discovered, they'd underestimated my agility and strength. I hadn't given them time to use their mind control on me.

Scholars weren't typically known to possess physical abilities like those of the warrior class, but I'd grown attached to those I'd treated. Especially Sia Jakkar. Unlike his twin brother, Sia Sakkar, he'd frowned on the dependency on the technology that had--from one suns-rise to the next--miraculously been created.

The construction of the impenetrable dome over Huren was the first real division of the crown. Sia Jakkar had preached to the warriors not to become dependent on the dome for protection, but to continue training, to keep their fighting skills honed.

Some chose to follow him, while others chose a more leisurely existence and sided with Sia Sakkar, as did the Royal Council--our decision-makers and law enforcers--had also chosen the decadent path.

As the Royal Medic, I served the crown. Both sides of it. Though I'd tried to remain neutral when it came to politics, I valued Sia Jakkar's principles more and viewed the division as just the beginning of nothing good, so I stayed close to Sia Jakkar and his warriors, even requested to be taught fighting skills in secret in case I ever had to defend myself.

Before anyone knew what was happening, Kayyot and I were sequestered, locked inside our palace rooms while Huren erupted into conflict. The crowns fragmented; two brothers torn apart because of what we all thought was a difference of opinion.

One remained as ruler, while the other was exiled along with his followers. We were told later, Sia Sakkar had ordered their executions. That was when the Gretolic's first showed their grotesque faces, and I knew Huren was doomed.

My lungs burned, my thighs cramped, but I refused to stop until I lost my pursuers. If I was caught, I'll meet the same fate as my colleague. Kayyot gave his life for the truth I had clutched in my hands. I would not allow his death to be in vain.

What we'd stumbled upon inside a secret lab had sent shards of ice shooting through my veins. As we'd collected the evidence of the Gretolics crimes against Valose, Kayyot had stood bravely against the ones who caught us in the act.

We'd fought back, taking down the Valosians under the spell of the Gretolics. More came before we could get away. Once we were overpowered, Kayyot created a distraction and put me in a position to flee. Then he'd tossed me the case and yelled at me to run just before the dagger was drawn across his throat.

I needed to get this into the hands of someone I trusted. The truth I carried would change everything, but Sia Jakkar was gone, and the enemy was everywhere.

There were only a few I knew I could turn to for help. At the end of the hall, I slid to a halt and pried open the door to the lift. The lift wasn't there. It sat a few floors above me inside the shaft.

I jumped down the open shaft in a split decision, falling fifteen floors with a twist of my knee. The snap of the joint ricocheted off the metal walls, as did my scream of agony.

Many voices rained down on my head. When I looked up, the beady eyes of the Gretolic glared down at me from around the doorway where I'd dropped.

Strength gathered with my refusal to give up, and I stood to pry open the lift door on the ground level. My flailing exit was anything but graceful. Thankfully, there was no one around to stop me.

I raced out the closet exit, careened around the corner of the palace, and slipped into the sewage drain that would eventually empty into a large underground holding tank.

I hobbled my way through the filth of the city. My knee

was screaming with every lopsided gait. Before I ended up in the tank, I veered right and forced myself to climb the ladder to the surface that led just outside Hexxus' cottage.

I had to find a way out of the dome and away from Huren. Hexxus was the only male that knew enough about the technology to help me. I also knew he had no love for the Gretolics.

"You smell of shit, Maxxon," Hexxus remarked in greeting.

"I have no time for games, scholar." I pushed my way inside his humble cottage and locked the door. "I need your help to get out of the dome."

His shrewd eyes narrowed on the case in my arms. "What have you gone and done, medic?"

"The less you know, the better off you are." I hopped to the window and peered out. Two of Sia Sakkar's portly warriors were just exiting the palace with a Gretolic on their heels. "Now, will you help me or not?"

The warriors were taking their sweet time searching for me--their faith in the dome to keep me trapped inside, absolute. Hopefully, the device Hexxus had been developing was operational. If not, I'd have to find another way out.

I shifted my weight, hopping on my good leg as I waited for Hexxus to answer. His gaze was wild as he stared me down.

Had I misread him? Was he not as trustworthy as I'd thought?

I knew he'd shouldered all the blame for the Gretolics infiltration of Clan Huren. The fault was not his alone to bear. However, he was doing everything he could to make things right again, yet the more time that passed, the more frazzled his appearance. As of late, I'd been worried about his mental stability.

Suddenly, Hexxus turned on his heel and pulled out a small box from a hatch hidden in the floor. Inside were circular devices. He handed me one with instructions on how to activate it.

"Once the light on the top comes on, place it on the dome." Hexxus demonstrated, turning the two halves of the device in opposite directions. "It will displace the dome's shielding, creating a portal. A fluctuation of energy will ripple the shielding and will alert the Gretolics, so once you're out, don't hesitate. Disappear into the jungle and get as far from here as you can."

"Come with me," I said as he places the device in my palm.

"I wish I could, but I have to remain here and find a way to stop the Gretolics." Hexxus closed my fingers around the device and clasped my fist in both his hands. "Get as far away from Huren as you can. Stay hidden, and don't come back until I ping you."

"Hexxus, no," I pleaded when he handed me a comm then began stuffing provisions into a pack. "You need to come with me. Huren is no longer safe for any of us."

"Don't concern yourself with me. I have a plan." He thrust the pack at me. "Take Kayyot with you--"

"Dead. Kayyot is dead," I spat the words. "Killed at the order of the Gretolics because of this." I held up the case.

Hexxus just stared at me, unblinking before clearing his throat. "I'm so sorry, Maxxon. I know he was like a brother to you."

My eyes dropped to the ground between us. What more could be said? The loss of a talented medic and a good male was a tragedy beyond words.

"Do not try and contact me. If you use the comm, the signal can be traced, and you'll be giving away your location."

Hexxus peeked through the windows of his cottage. "So, wait for me to contact you when it's safe to return. Keep your found secret hidden and trust no one."

"I won't." I held the case tighter to my chest and shouldered the pack.

"With any luck from the Spirits, you'll hear from me soon." Hexxus nudged me toward the door. "All is clear. Now go! Run and don't come back until I ping you."

"Hexxus--"

"You're wasting precious time arguing." Hexxus opened the door and shoved me out. "Now go!" He slammed the door shut in my face.

"Fucking Helios! Good luck, my friend," I whispered the last and limped as fast as I could toward the warrior training field.

After Sia Jakkar was dethroned by his twin brother, and all of his warriors had gone with him, the field had lain barren. It should be the safest place to exit the dome. And I wanted to arm myself before running headlong into a deadly jungle.

I barely made it to the armory before the strange, white crafts began to land in the center of the training field. I hugged the building, peering around the corner as they lined up one beside the other. A single Gretolic flew each one.

Where had they come from?

I looked to the sky for answers, only to be greeted with the twin suns' glint off the dome's top. A final craft zoomed out of Sia Sakkar's hanger, swooping down over the few civilians allowed to roam the city streets.

Curfews and lockdowns had been implemented after Sia Jakkar had stood against his brother. Civilian and warrior class alike had been rounded up, everyone questioned to determine their allegiance to which crown.

Few were allowed to freely roam the city--most being

laborers and craftsmen going about their work. The warriors remained mainly inside the palace, close to Sia Sakkar. I do not know what became of the others.

Our misfortunes had started as a pair. First the catastrophic war with the Nuttaki, then another brutal hit when our females perished from a germ I could not stop. Nonetheless, our clan had stayed strong, banded together despite the tragic loss.

That was when we had twin rulers to bind us as one clan. And no interference from otherworldly visitors to hold influence over our council members.

I gritted my teeth and clutched the case in my hands. What I had inside here would change everything if I could get it in the right hands. For now, I would have to wait, bide my time, and hide the truth until Hexxus pinged my comm.

I hardly recognized this Huren. What lay before me now was a city on its deathbed, ready to breathe its final, agonal breath.

The Gretolics cleared the field, leaving their crafts behind. I punched in the code, and the door to the armory clicked open. Inside was dark, but my nocturnal lenses were only a blink away.

I passed the racks of training swords lined up in the center of the room and went right for the battle swords hanging so magnificently on the walls.

Valosian steel. There was nothing like it in all the world. Sleek and resilient, the two-edged blades gleamed with the promise of death.

I chose a harness and hurriedly donned it, sheathing my swords to crisscross over my back. Before leaving, I paused to look around at the deadly weapons waiting to be used to defend our people.

This couldn't be it. After all we'd endured, the end of a

great and mighty clan could not be at the frail hands of the little gray monsters. I wouldn't allow it.

My nature was to heal, not to fight. With a final inhale of the metallic-tinged air, the desire for war raced through my blue blood. This surge of bloodlust must be what the warriors felt as they readied for battle. For the first time in my life, the desire to kill rode me hard.

I cracked the door enough to see the field beyond. The twin suns were setting in a perfect, cloudless sky. Brilliant streaks of blue and silver lit up the world in a fiery farewell.

The training field was void of life. I touched the device that Hexxus had given me in the pocket of my kiltus. Now was my chance.

I slipped out and crept close to the armory wall until I reached the backside, closest to the dome's perimeter. My knee throbbed with every step.

I fingered the device in my pocket and stared into the thick vegetation that would hide my trail as well as place me in danger. The shielding was the only thing keeping the jungle and all its beasts at bay. Once I crossed that translucent barrier, I would be victim to what lay beyond.

I stood a chance with two good legs, but injured and alone? I might as well lay myself out like a buffet.

My head swiveled over to the aliens' crafts lined up in the field. Their dull, white bodies reflected none of the suns' dying rays. Oval in shape, they had no top. I'd seen the Gretolics rolling a large ball embedded in the console while turning another to maneuver the craft.

I hopped to the nearest craft and climbed inside. "If those slinky little shits can fly this contraption, then so can I," I said to myself with a quick glance around.

No one was around, and the city was growing darker by the sec. I tossed the pack Hexxus had given me onto the seat next to me and tucked the case close to my side as I squeezed my large frame into the driver's seat.

With a deep breath, I rolled the ball embedded in the center of the console beneath my hand and braced for movement. "Fucking *Helios*!" I cursed the Realm of the Wicked when nothing happened.

"There has to be something..." I swept my eyes over the slick interior, turned the knob to the side, and still nothing.

I let loose a string of obscenities that would have made any seasoned warrior proud and pushed a button hidden under the console.

The craft shot up into the air, plastering me back into the cramped seat. I slapped my palm over the ball and rolled it away from myself, which shot me forward and kept me from crashing into the top of the dome.

Now I was heading into the curved wall ahead. I turned the knob over on the side, and the craft slowed to a more manageable speed. Now that I'd slowed, I looked down at the audience beginning to gather below me.

They knew where I was now. Going by the sneers on the Gretolics faces, they were not happy about me commandeering their craft.

The craft wobbled and sped up as I made adjustments to the knob. I rolled the ball and moved back and forth, rocked and slowed. I must look ridiculous trying to maneuver this thing, like a youngling trying to drive his first rover.

I was getting the hang of it—well, maybe. I dipped, then rightened the craft before I dumped myself out onto the ground.

Shit got critical when the Gretolics ran for their crafts and came after me with a practiced ease that flashed my scales an angry blue. I fumbled along with my stolen craft, keeping just enough distance between myself and the enemy.

I thrust my hand in my pocket and pulled out the device

Hexxus gave me. I had to go hands-free on the craft to twist the device and activate it. The craft lurched, and the light blinked on just as Hexxus showed me.

Now to figure out how to attach the device while flying the craft. This was going to be a trick.

The Gretolics were gaining on me fast while I careened through the air over the city. I swooped past the palace, narrowly missing one of the terraces on the upper levels. It would be a beautiful scene under different circumstances.

Now was not the time for sight-seeing. Palming the device, I lurched past an oncoming Gretolic. His craft listed hard to one side to miss my wobbling craft. I didn't look back to see if he recovered but rolled the ball full speed ahead and threw Hexxus's device at the dome's wall and prayed to the Spirits I made it through in one piece.

The device hit the dome in an outward, resonating ripple, yet the shield still looked wholly intact. I was going to slam into the dome's wall.

With a sudden flash, I was hit with a fresh jungle breeze. The portal presented as a small circle but still large enough for the craft to fly through. I lined up my craft the best I could and ducked down, flying through the hole with a bobble.

Once I cleared the dome, I chanced a backward glance. The device flashed, fell from the dome, and closed the portal. The Gretolics following me didn't have a chance to stop. Their bulbous heads exploded upon impact. Their crafts crumpled in a puff of dark smoke.

I faced forward with a smile and breathed deeply of the fresh air. I hadn't realized, living inside the confines of the dome, how stagnant the air had become.

As I flew over the jungle and peered down over the dense foliage, Valose looked so serene from up here. The world indeed was breathtaking from this lofty height.

I glanced around while trying to fly straight, searching for wetlocks, giant winged predators that might view me as a snack. Lucky for me, none appeared to be emerging from their nests even though the twin suns had set.

The dome sheltering Huren grew smaller and smaller as I plotted a course toward the west that would take me away from the city. Hexxus had said to get as far away as I could. Where in Helios could I go?

With my dark penetrating lenses covering my eyes, I peered through the darkness at the jungle below. There was no safe place on the ground.

After many hurs of flying I came upon the floratrap fields and the edge of the Nuttaki's territory. I veered a little north, skirting the Jurigon Mountains and over the back entrance to the Caverns of the Ancients.

Light from the full moon shimmered over the uninhabited island chain in the Haydian Sea. I chose the largest landmass out of the four and swallowed hard, sending up a prayer to the Spirits that I crossed the churning waters without a squidlin plucking me from the air.

My hands shook as I clumsily navigated the craft over the sea toward the islands. I'd never been up this high before and never over a body of water this large and opposing.

We only knew of the squidlin with their gaping jaws and long, gangly tentacles, which was why no one bothered to venture out to sea. The adventurous few who had, never made it far before being snatched and dragged beneath the churning waves, never to be seen again. What else lay beneath those dark waters was anyone's guess.

With the island beneath me, I searched for a place to land. "That looks promising," I mumbled to myself and began my shaky descent over a flat stretch of barren earth.

I tugged the button under the console, and the ground rushed up to meet me, so I eased off. The controls were touchy. I'd have to learn to make minor adjustments, so I didn't get myself killed.

My landing was jarring, but at least I didn't crash the vehicle. I'd need it again to get off this chunk of land as soon as Hexxus pinged me.

I exited the craft. My injured knee buckled as I stood on new ground. The air was balmy with a hint of salt from the constant breeze wafting in from the Haydian Sea.

I tucked the case into the waistband of my kiltus and shouldered the pack over my sword harness. I worried the craft had some kind of tracking device. I'd leave it here, out in the open during the dark hurs and see if anyone showed up looking for it.

As for myself--I eyed the small mountain in the center of the island. Up looked like a good option to pass the dark hurs. To my knowledge, these islands had never been explored. I had no way of knowing what, if anything, inhabited this land.

I moved cautiously, with my knee protesting every step as I made my way around the base of the peak until I found a place to start my ascent. I picked my way up rocky steps that appeared to be a natural staircase in the side of the mountain. I encountered little vegetation but found many small caves on my way to the top.

At the pinnacle, I stood in awe of the panoramic view. The Haydian Sea crashed all around in a salty froth. Small creatures jumped out of the churning waters in carefree arcs. I wondered what else lived below the dark waters beside the terrifying squidlin.

I took shelter in a small cave just below the peak to wait out the dark hurs. I breathed in a taste of freedom for the first time since the dome was built. Despite the vulnerability of living with the dangers of the jungle's beasts, housed like a specimen under a translucent prison defeated the purpose of living without fear.

What we feared the most had been living inside with us the entire time.

Amazon

Map of Valose

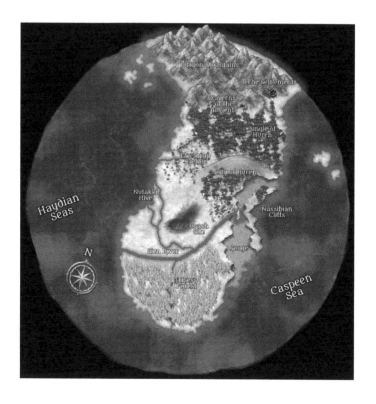

Also by Iona Strom

Nomadican Mates Series

Nomadican Mates Series Mega Box Set (books 1-7): Sci-Fi Alien
Abduction Romance

Alien Intervention Romance

Zaku: Alien Intervention Romance book 1

Coming Soon!

Warriors of Valose Saga

Silver Savage: Warriors of Valose Saga 1

Silver Seducer: Warriors of Valose Saga 2

Silver Savior: Warriors of Valose Saga 3

Silver Solace: Warriors of Valose Saga 4

Silver Scout: Warriors of Valose Saga 5

Silver Silence: Warriors of Valose Saga 6

Silver Spice: Warriors of Valose Saga 7

Silver Storm: Warriors of Valose Saga 8

Silver Steel: Warriors of Valose Saga 9

Silver Stealth: Warrior of Valose Saga 10

More Warriors to Come!

Also by LS Anders

Exotic Ink Series

Exotic Ink Series Bundle Books 1-3

Mythical Ink Series

Mythical Ink Series Bundle Books 1-3
A Fairy's Tale: Mythical Ink Series Book 4

Men of Measure Series

Six Pack: Men of Measure Book 1

About the Authors

Stalk the Authors!

Iona Strom writes for readers who love hot, erotic romance featuring exotic alien males who believe human females are a delicacy to be devoured—over and over again.

Don't miss out on Sales and New Releases when you join Iona's Readers Group.

Treat yourself to exclusive Sneak Peeks of upcoming books by signing up for Iona's Newsletter!

Follow Iona's Amazon Author Page and get the latest news about her books directly from Amazon!

Follow Iona on BookBub!

Follow Iona on TikTok!

LS Anders is a spinner of tales and dirty of mind. Author of contemporary and paranormal romance, she decided to dip her toes in the world of sci-fi romance to bring you the naughtiest tales imaginable.

Follow LS Anders Amazon Author Page and get the latest news about her books directly from Amazon!

Follow LS Anders on BookBub!

Made in the USA
Coppell, TX
09 May 2022

77605861R00104